A LADY LOVES MUCH

BROTHERS OF BELLE FOURCHE: BOOK 7

KARI TRUMBO

INKED IN FAITH PUBLICATIONS

A Lady Loves Much

Copyright © 2019 Kari Trumbo

All rights reserved.

ISBN: 9781092748964

All rights reserved under International and Pan-American Copyright Conventions

This is a work of fiction. Names, characters, places, and incidents are either the products of the author's imagination or are used fictitiously, and any resemblance to actual persons, living or dead, business establishments, events, or locales is purely coincidental.

No part of this book may be reproduced or transmitted in any form or by any electronic or mechanical means, including photocopying, recording or by any information storage and retrieval system, without the written permission of the publisher, except where permitted by law.

Cover design by Carpe Librum Book Design

FROM THE BACK COVER

George covers his fear of loss by trying to be as much of a man as he can.

As a boy, he lost his mother and feels like it's his fault. He doesn't want to find a wife, she would be just another woman for him to lose. When he seeks the attention of the new poetry teacher, it's only to have a good story to tell the other hands. Unfortunately, every time he gets near her, he can't think of anything but poetry.

Phoebe Root believes if she doesn't spread a love of poetry, the art will die.

When a cowboy casually enters her class and shocks her with his reaction to her poetry, she can't give up on him.

An illness settles over Belle Fourche, as dangerous as the one that took George's mother. Will he let her go to avoid another loss, or hold tight and claim his first love?

⁹ And he said unto me, My grace is sufficient for thee: for my strength is made perfect in weakness. Most gladly therefore will I rather glory in my infirmities, that the power of Christ may rest upon me.
¹⁰ Therefore I take pleasure in infirmities, in reproaches, in necessities, in persecutions, in distresses for Christ's sake: for when I am weak, then am I strong.
2 Corinthians 12:9-10

CHAPTER 1

Belle Fourche, South Dakota
October, 1902

George Oleson squared his shoulders and concentrated as he slowly made his way to the little white school in the distance. Horses exhaled puffs of warm breath into the night and the whistle of a train screamed in the distance. He didn't come to town often, but he'd decided it was time to start acting his age. Miss Root at the little school would help him to do just that.

He was a man now, and men were supposed to make women fan their faces and giggle. He doubted he would find a fan within a hundred miles in the chill of the October evening. But still, he should be the topic of some woman's conversation, someone who would smile at the mention of his name. All the men in the bunkhouse had made it sound like he wouldn't be a man until that happened and since his brothers had both made their matches in the last few months, he was inclined to believe them.

Miss Phoebe Root was in that school, reading her poetry to the town. He'd tried before, when she was at the boarding house and the prior week at the reading, to wave and catch her attention, but she'd done her best to ignore him. This week, he'd made up his mind to speak to her, sure that she'd practically swoon right into his arms. He was man enough for that to happen. Then he'd have a story to tell.

He put on his best saunter as he fixed his Sunday tie and ignored the whisper of doubt in the back of his mind. She'd arrived in Belle Fourche a week before and time was short for her to notice him. Cowboys all over town were talking about her hair, so deep red it was more like a warm brown, and her shy smile. There wasn't a one of them who weren't smitten.

Except him. George wasn't smitten, he just wanted to be sure he had it in him to catch the eye of a woman if he ever cared to. Miss Root just happened to be the one he'd chosen. He'd known from the moment he set eyes on her that she would respond to him. That's all this was. A little game. Just like all the other games he played. He teased people, pushed them until they were angry, then laughed it off. He was the jokester, prankster. He'd made his sister's life miserable after Mama had died, and he couldn't even bring himself to feel sorry for it. It was better for Natalie that she not like him. Just like he wouldn't get close to the teacher. The story for the other men wouldn't be as good if he got hog-tied by a woman.

He pressed closer to the school. The warm glow made the shadows nearby seem even deeper. He stalled, closing his eyes. What was he doing? What if she *did* fall for his charms? What if she somehow made it past his defenses? His laugh lacked any humor and he shook his head as he strode up the stairs for the door. She was just a woman—weak. She would never get through to him. He wouldn't let her.

He yanked the door open and Miss Root sat on a stool in the front of everyone, her long dark skirts were tucked lightly around her, accentuating her small frame. Droves of people crushed into all the little desks and in seats wherever they could find room. There was only one narrow aisle up the center to where she sat on the little dais, making her easier to see. She stopped her reading and her soft face glanced up and met his eyes. His heart clenched painfully and he froze, door in hand, as her dark, gentle gaze locked his knees in place. She was a beauty. A lady in every sense of the word. Better than any other woman in town and certainly better than any he'd met.

"Why don't you come in and close the door?" Her voice was soft, yet persuasive, and he found himself doing her bidding without even thinking.

He closed the door and stood there, unable to stop staring at her, clutching the door as if he needed a hold on something real. Though he felt lots of other eyes on him, he didn't even care to see who they were. Miss Root delicately cleared her throat and bent her head over the book once more. Her voice rose and fell in soft and gentle waves, then built with more power than he expected out of her. The words slid past his ears and drove deep within him. Meaningless, yet grave. Some crashed around inside him, heavier than others, then were soon replaced by the next swell. All that mattered was the emotion on her face and the sound of her voice. He was powerless to move.

The poem slowed, a gentle eddy in a pond, then came to an end and everyone in the school clapped, breaking him out of his spell. He wanted to yell at them to hush, they were ruining it. There was supposed to be silence, he could feel it and they didn't understand. She had created this place of mystery like he'd never known and they'd yanked it away.

"Now that you've seen how it's done, with speed and inflection, perhaps one of my students would like to try? Millie, you've been doing your studies, how about you?" Miss Root stood and handed the book off to his neighbor.

Millie accepted the book and flounced her skirt as she took the stool, but George's eyes followed Miss Root as she made her way to the back of the room, just a few feet from him. While he'd been completely under the influence of Miss Root's poem, he easily ignored Millie's. From Miss Root's close proximity, he could see the soft glints of bright red in her hair. She held her arm across her stomach, as if to protect herself, and her head was bent, giving her the look of a shy school girl who had aged to that of a teacher, but had never learned the confidence to go with it.

She was purely lovely, and his tongue was as tied as a lassoed calf.

He swallowed hard and forced himself to close his eyes. What was he doing? He didn't want a woman to complicate his life and she didn't want a smart-mouthed cowboy giving her trouble. He needed to just leave. He sucked in a deep breath and turned to go.

Someone touched his arm, so light he almost missed it, and he turned. She was there, not feet away, but right next to him. Her scent was something rich and deep that he'd never smelled before. Her eyes were big, the deepest blue, and as expressive as her voice had been.

"Please, don't go just now. If you do, you'll interrupt her reading. She's doing so well."

He stood for a moment, speechless, staring at her hand on his arm. His heart clamored for his attention. Blast it all, he was supposed to make *her* feel that way, not the other way around. He nodded and turned back to pretend to watch Millie, but now that Miss Root was right there, his mind was a lost cause.

PHOEBE SURREPTITIOUSLY GLANCED at the cowboy standing next to her. He certainly was a fine looking man, and quite surprising. She'd caught his eyes shining, as if he'd really *felt* her poem earlier. None of the other cowboys in the room had done that. They hardly managed to look like they could stand to pay attention. The only look they afforded her was that of desire. She had no time for them.

She'd learned in school she was adept at poetry and public speaking. To turn that into a job, she'd registered as a teacher and traveled from school to school, working with teachers to help students learn the importance of poetry and the confidence in their own voices. Her teachers had all said it was a dying art and she couldn't let that happen. If there was no room for poetry, where would that leave her? Her heart spoke to her in poetic tones and language was her dearest friend. No one in life really understood her.

He adjusted his weight to one hip next to her, his forehead furrowed. While he'd taken in her reading with interest, Millie had no such hold. He shifted his weight back and forth, frowned, and glanced all over the room. While Millie was still learning, she didn't have the art down yet, the emotion needed to bring a listener into the poem. She wanted to say something to help him understand he should stay, should learn more, but she held back. He could be just another cowboy. There was no way to know for certain.

Millie finished and the room clapped softly. Her little face beamed—the girl did love attention. She'd recently turned thirteen and the Nicksons had held a great party for her. Though the Nicksons had many children, Millie seemed to be the apple of their eye. Millie glanced over the crowd, then found Phoebe. "Shall I read another, Miss Root?"

Heavens no. Not until she'd had more classes. Phoebe wanted the people of Belle Fourche to keep coming to her weekly poetry readings and classes, which meant she had to keep their interest and make them take part. "No, thank you, Millie." Phoebe pushed away from the wall and strode up the center aisle. Though she could feel many sets of eyes on her, those of the cowboy she'd just left behind seemed to penetrate deeper, as if her very soul knew the touch of his.

She took the book from Millie and handed it to the girl's mother, to continue. The room felt stuffy with everyone pressed inside. Phoebe grabbed the small slate Stephenia used during class and used it as a fan. Her face burned hot as the sun as three more people took their turns. Though she waited to see if the cowboy in the back would read, he didn't come forward.

"I would like to remind everyone that I'm holding classes here every Friday after school from four o'clock until six. Bring a dish for all to share and we'll eat while we learn. The weekly reading will follow. Thank you all for coming. I'm so proud of my students." She never knew how to end a night. It wasn't like her to be without words, but saying goodbye was always the hardest part. When the room emptied, then she would have nothing to do until the following Friday. Goodbye always meant loneliness for an entire week.

The room slowly emptied with many of the people wanting to speak to her. The married women were looking for companionship and a way to stimulate their minds, the students wanted to impress her and get a good grade. The cowboys wanted attention with puffing out their chests and false words of flattery, laughing, posturing. She answered them quickly and sent them on their way, as they punched each other's arms and joked back and forth.

Soon, it was just Stephenia Oleson who was the Belle Fourche school teacher, the cowboy who'd caught her attention earlier, and herself in the school. Stephenia strode to the stove and opened the door, grabbing the metal scoop and slowly banking the coals. "I'll take care of this, Phoebe. Do you have all of your bags from the boarding house?"

The cowboy's eyes widened. "You're leaving? I thought you just had a bunch of people sign up for your class?" Though his words sounded like an accusation, his face merely showed confusion.

Her heart wanted to understand the confused man, to know why he stayed behind. She pushed that hope of finally finding a kindred spirit to the abyss that was the back of her mind. No rural cowboy could fill that ache for someone who could understand her. She strode forward and held out her hand. "I'm Miss Phoebe Root, from Michigan. I've signed a contract with the Belle Fourche school to teach poetry over the winter. I'm not going anywhere, just moving out of the boarding house. For the amount of time the school board wants me to stay, it's costly for them to rent a room. So, Mr. and Mrs. Oleson offered to take me in for the winter. It works well since Stephenia is the teacher here and lives on the same ranch."

He didn't release his hold on her and his touch was warm and strong, though not as bold as she'd first assumed he would be. His eyes didn't leave hers and the longer he held both her gaze and her fingers, the more nervous energy built within her and she wanted to pull away.

Stephenia laughed softly. "He knows exactly who I am."

His shoulders relaxed slightly. "I'm George Oleson." He bent to kiss her hand.

Phoebe tugged her hand free of his before his lips could come near her. While he was rare in that poetry seemed to touch him, he wasn't rare enough to let him near her. She had to keep on teaching students and that required focus.

"Mr. Oleson, it would seem that I'll be living on the same ranch as you then. Stephenia tells me there's plenty of room out there. I'm happy to have a place to stay that's so close to her."

He ducked his head for a moment. When he glanced back up at her, the warm eyes she'd seen earlier were gone, replaced by those of all the other men who'd come to see her that night. She stepped back from him slightly. But why should she be surprised? Hadn't Robert done just the same? He'd pretended to feel, he'd pretended to take an interest in everything she did, until she'd almost married him. Only after she'd agreed had she realized it was a lie, and she'd left. Almost too late.

He puffed out his chest and she couldn't stand for him to ruin the illusion just yet. "Mr. Oleson, why don't you consider signing up for my class? I think you might really hold some promise."

Stephenia chuckled from the stove behind her and she saw the slash of hurt and anger in his eyes as his pride was dented.

"Nope, I only came for the pretty scenery." He touched his hat, turned on his heel, and walked away.

So, was he as confused as he'd seemed at first? Did George run deeper than she thought, and certainly deeper than Stephenia thought? She'd been sure she'd seen emotion in him, more than anyone else in the room had shown, but her doubts closed off her ears.

"Stay away from that one, Phoebe. He's a braggart and a trickster. I don't know what possessed him to come tonight, but I'll talk to Nathen about making sure he doesn't bother you anymore."

"No," she answered too quickly, still in her own thoughts. "I mean, I don't want to prevent anyone from getting some good out of my classes. Even if they only come to the readings. I'll ask him to stop coming *if* he becomes a problem."

"Oh, he will. Mark my words." Stephenia began extinguishing the lamps in the window ledges.

Phoebe's gaze held on the door as if he might come back through it. She would teach him to see and hear poetry as it was meant to be, then she would send him on his way, just like she did with every other student. Because she was a teacher, and that was what was expected of her. Trouble or not.

CHAPTER 2

Stephenia sat stiffly next to Phoebe on the seat of the buckboard. Her small trunk lay just behind them. The teacher hadn't said a word to her since she'd admonished Phoebe to stay away from George. Her defense of the cowboy had turned the teacher on her. A cloud hung between them that Phoebe wanted to dispel right away.

"I know you mean well, and I know you know George better than I do. But would you exclude students from learning, simply because they aren't easy to teach?"

If it was possible, Stephenia sat even more rigid. "It isn't like that at all. You *do* have a choice in whom you teach. I don't. George Oleson is trouble. I don't think he means to be hurtful, but he truly is. Arnold and his brothers have tried so hard to get through to him, but it just isn't possible."

She nodded to make Stephenia assume she'd taken

her words to heart, but the opposite was true. Her words made Phoebe long to reach him all the more. He *had* been touched by the poem. Why else would he have stayed if he was so unreachable? She'd been teaching long enough to know now when someone cared and when they didn't. Just thinking about it bolstered her hope. A lingering doubt whispered about her past failure with Robert, but she blinked it away. She was older now, wiser.

"Be that as it may, I'd like to give him the opportunity. Give me a reason other than your word why I shouldn't allow him to join in on a town function. He behaved himself tonight." Unlike some of the other men whom she wished she could have asked to leave.

Stephenia flicked the lines and Phoebe wrapped her blanket tighter over her legs as the wind whipped at her. The evening air in October was chilly, just like home. She'd been warned the snow could pile deep in that area of South Dakota. The doctor had said, once she was there, she'd best plan to stay for the entire winter. Dr. Spight, who ran the Belle Fourche school board, had offered to keep her there for his students and for her safety.

"Do you struggle with making it to school during the winter months?" Phoebe wanted to change the direction of their chat away from one which obviously bothered her new friend.

"Sometimes. Though, if I can't make it in, neither can many of my students. Dr. Spight lives right in town and if the weather is so poor I can't get in, he lets everyone who made it know to go back home, after he's made sure they're warm enough."

The doctor had seemed like a man who genuinely cared about the children, so it didn't surprise Phoebe to know he would light a fire in the school stove just to let students warm up before sending them back home, even if they only lived a few blocks away. "I will only need to come in on Fridays, but if you'd like any help I would be glad to offer."

Stephenia smiled slightly. "Be careful, if you're too willing the school board might grant you a position. They might be needing one soon enough."

Phoebe had suspected, with Stephenia's short temper, that she was in a family way. Though she hadn't come out and said it, there was no other reason she would leave the position she loved. They were too new as friends to offer much more than a congratulations, but lately, whenever Phoebe had been approached by women in a family way, she'd felt a pull inside. Nothing drastic, just a tug on her heart that hadn't been there before. "I'm sure you'll want to continue even with a baby on your hip."

Stephenia gave a stiff smile. "It's really too early to know for sure and, while that might be true, the school board has its limits. They allow teachers to be married, but once we have children, we're expected to stay home with them. Part of me finds it unjust, because I'm sure Maretta had to do all her work once she had Conrad. She wasn't relieved of any of her duties, in fact, new ones were added with the care of an infant. Another part of me is glad I won't be forced to make a choice, because while I love my students, they are not mine." She directed the wagon through a large gate onto a long entrance. The house and buildings were little more than a speck, they were so far off.

"My, I've never lived anywhere quite so…forlorn." A chill raced up her arms and down her spine. The town had seemed small amid the vast land surrounding it, but this little clump of houses and barns seemed to be fighting a losing battle against the lonely prairie.

"There's nothing forlorn about it. It's wonderful and peaceful out here. Maretta will keep you busy all day long and Wilhelmina is there to talk to. She's only a year or so younger than you."

"Oh? Wilhelmina Galliger, from the boarding house?" She'd talked to the woman a few times. Though Will, as she preferred to be called, wasn't like Phoebe in the slightest, they had been able to converse easily.

"Yes, that's her. Charles, George's brother, is courting her right now. They intend to have a small herd together."

Phoebe laughed, because she made it sound like the cattle would be their family. "Is that so? I'll be sure to send them a letter of congratulations."

Stephenia finally pulled the wagon to a stop in front of a huge white house with black shutters and a full porch all around the front, leading to the back on one side. It was even bigger than the boarding house and much more welcoming.

"My goodness." Phoebe couldn't help but stare.

Homes had been getting larger and larger as they'd moved into the eighteenth century, but this one wasn't new. It had the feel of having been there for many years with mature lilacs and flower beds surrounding it.

George strode out to meet them, undeterred by his earlier failure to kiss her hand, and Stephenia's sharp tongue. Warmth crept up her cheeks. He held out his hand to help her down and she accepted it. Another man, who was quite obviously another Oleson, followed and helped Stephenia down then kissed her on the forehead and whispered something in her ear. He went for the team and Stephenia lingered, though she glanced after her husband, obviously wanting to follow.

"Wait!" Phoebe called, "My trunk!"

George smirked slightly and was there before she could even move, lifting her trunk from the back and hefting it toward the house. "I'll let Aunt Maretta know you're here." He strode past her and off into the house, leaving her feeling all alone.

Stephenia was silent for a moment as they both stared after him. "I've never seen him do a single thing for anyone else. He only cooks in the bunkhouse when it's his day, he only does extra chores if asked, and he never backs down from a disagreement."

Phoebe pursed her lips slightly, but couldn't voice aloud what was going through her mind, because Stephenia wouldn't understand. Only those who heard poetry in their hearts could.

The trunk wasn't all that heavy, but Uncle Nathen had made him leave it in the kitchen all the same, saying he'd bring it up to whatever room Aunt Maretta wanted later. He'd given George his stern eye for even asking. That eye had kept him from doing many things since they'd arrived in Belle Fourche five months before. He'd learned he didn't necessarily need to bow to his uncle, but he did have to learn from him.

He itched to understand who he was, because he didn't like who he thought he was. Every new experience left him changed, but unsure. Maybe, as he got older, he could become someone else, someone better. As he strode back out to the bunkhouse, a chill came over his skin and he remembered the worst night of his life from ten years before.

Mama had been so sick. Everyone had been so grave and serious, taking turns bathing her forehead with damp cloths, even him. He'd only been eleven, but he'd wanted to help Mama get better. He'd prayed while dripping water over her hot skin, but nothing seemed to work. They'd tried everything they knew. He'd helped by going to nearby farms and getting buckets of water as they ran out. Everything they'd asked of him, he'd done.

When his oldest brother John had taken over after his turn one night, George had snuck out. Since they lived out of their wagon, they came across many people and he'd remembered traveling through an

Indian encampment. They couldn't afford a doctor, but maybe the Indians had someone who could help Mama? He'd begged to speak to someone, though no one seemed to know his language. Finally, he'd met with someone who could understand him and the Medicine Man had sent a pouch of herbs. He hadn't even bothered to come and talk to George, merely sent the small sack with the person who could speak English. The man had warned him it wouldn't work. He'd told George it only worked for *his people*. But George had taken it back to Mama and tried it anyway.

He'd mixed the herbs with water the next day and dribbled it down her throat while it was his turn to sit with her, praying she would get better. She'd barely noticed him and only flinched slightly at the taste. Her fever spiked a few hours later, and she was gone before morning. Even though he knew better than to think it was his fault—she'd already been sick—he couldn't shake that weight. He'd tried and failed to save Mama.

When Natalie had tried to take Mama's place, he'd lit into her with all his anger, all his hostility, every hurt he couldn't speak aloud. She had no right. Mama's place was an important one and no sister could do the job. It didn't matter that his horrible words and treatment didn't bring Mama back, and he was sure it didn't help Natalie. He simply couldn't love the girl who tried to replace Mama.

Pa had never been the same after Mama died. Though he had his own grief to deal with, he never looked at George again, not any of the boys. He didn't even pretend to be a pa. Maybe he'd known about George's foolish attempt to save Ma and was disappointed. There was no way to know now. He'd died in July and hadn't bothered to say anything to his sons beforehand, despite knowing he was sick.

Natalie was now married and lived just outside of Belle Fourche. John, his oldest brother, was also married and had gone a few weeks before to work a horse ranch he'd inherited from his wife's grandfather. Charles had fallen for a woman who everyone thought was a man. She'd even stayed in the bunkhouse, but now she lived with Uncle Nathen and Aunt Maretta until they could set a wedding date.

All his family was gone. He was alone.

That had to be why, even after such a failure to get Miss Root to notice him, he still wanted to catch her eye. It was why he'd watched for the wagon and helped immediately. He'd realized while riding home that his parting words to her were less than glowing. A woman probably didn't want to be known just for her looks. He certainly didn't want to be known for his cannon-fire attitude, yet, that's exactly why Stephenia had laughed when Miss Root had suggested he sign up for her class. He wasn't fool enough to deny it.

Charles met him at the door of the bunkhouse. "You just come from the house?"

He nodded, wanting to get in from the chill and away from freezing cold recollections. "Yes. And no, I didn't see Will." That was all Charles ever asked about anymore. He talked to their cousins about ranching, herd size, breeds, all the important things, but he never talked to George about important things, not since Will.

"You decided on a breed yet?" He wanted to test his brother, see if what he thought was true. Would Charles bother to even talk to him, or just shrug him off as someone who knew nothing?

"Not yet, I'm still considering. Conrad has ideas of what might work well for both of our herds, though mine will be much smaller and Will has a notion or two about what she'd like."

He hadn't even bothered to mention which breeds were being considered. George's shoulders tensed and he jammed his hands into his coat pockets. "Is it so hard to talk to me about these things? You're always rushing off to the house to talk to Will or over to Conrad's place to discuss things with him. You aren't married yet."

Charles laughed and scratched the back of his neck as he stepped back further in to the bunkhouse. "Not yet, but soon. The only reason I'm not out living on John's homestead is because the bunkhouse is closer to Will. Once she's ready, we'll both be out there. We have a lot to talk about before spring. Once calving season starts, we'll be able to start our herd."

What self-respecting woman wanted a herd? He'd never met anyone like it until Wilhelmina Galliger. "Do you include Will in *all* this herd talk? Since you say it's half hers."

Charles clapped him on the shoulder and laughed. "Of course. I don't want her getting angry with me. She has a good head on her shoulders and good ideas.

We can't use all of them, but we're equal partners. Some people think I'm a fool for doing it this way, but it was the only way I could show Will what a marriage could be like. She was willing to start a ranch with me, but afraid to spend a life with me. By showing her we can do this together, I've shown her we'll be good together."

George hadn't thought about that. It stuck in his craw that she had somehow managed to fool everyone into thinking she was strong. But women weren't, they were supposed to be frail and weak. God had made them that way. Wasn't Mama proof enough of that? She'd birthed and raised four children, then one little sickness took her away.

It bothered him that Will had been in the bunkhouse and heard the way men acted when women weren't supposed to be around. She'd fooled everyone, even if they now claimed she didn't. That made no sense. He'd been fooled completely. After living with men so long, it was no wonder she'd been unwilling to wed at first. Then again, what man would want to change his ways if he didn't have to?

His brothers had both changed when they'd met their women, but George didn't want to change. Living in the bunkhouse and playing cards with the men every night was an enjoyable pastime, especially on Friday nights. He rubbed his hands together, excited to start his evening. He liked being free after a long week of work to do as he pleased. A woman would mean he'd have to stop funning around and grow up. He was only twenty-one. Why should he have to?

Charles slapped his hat on his head and pulled on his gloves. "All the others decided to go into town for a night off. It's up to you to keep the stove burning at least until I get back." He secured the door behind him, leaving George all alone.

He groaned as he glanced around the empty, nearly dark room. A Friday night with no one to talk to wouldn't be much fun at all.

CHAPTER 3

Phoebe sat next to the fire in the sitting room and tried to read, but wasn't able to put herself into it like usual. She'd been taught if she didn't show a love of poetry to willing listeners, the art might die. Somewhere, on this ranch, was another person with the potential love of poetry, and she could do nothing about it. George was out there, working, when he could be buried in a book of poetry and brightening the confusion that darkened his eyes. She was a teacher, wasn't it her job to teach?

Will came in and sat across from her, crossing her leg at the knee. She was an unexpected woman who often sat and acted like a man, including spitting occasionally and crossing her arms across her chest. She even used a rifle for sport, not merely hunting. The woman was a pure enigma, which completely baffled and mildly repulsed Phoebe, who didn't know how to act around her.

"It's getting chilly out there," Will said in an attempt to make conversation as she leaned forward and glanced out the bank of windows in front of the house.

It wouldn't do to be rude. The woman was still a woman underneath all those manly tendencies. She *was* planning to marry Charles, so there had to be a woman in there somewhere. "Yes, the fire in here is quite nice. Would you like some tea?" She denoted the service setting on the small table. It was probably still warm.

"No, I only drink coffee, but thank you." Will stood back up and braced her hands at her hips. "Ever since I arrived in South Dakota, I wanted a piece of it all my own. I can't believe it will happen."

After Robert had used her own love against her, Phoebe was always careful to believe anything was meant to be before it actually occurred. "You're certain. He isn't just telling you all these things so you'll marry him?"

Will laughed, not the slightest bit offended by Phoebe's frank question. "Of course. I can't know for sure, but Charles is an honest man. Probably the most honest one I've ever met, and every day he shows me we can be partners. He asks my opinion and trusts my word. I don't try to take his job, and he doesn't make my portion less important. I don't need to steal his steam to make my fire."

She'd heard a rumor that Will had dressed as a man and even lived as one for a time and that made sense, given her manly ways. "Is it true that you used to wear trousers?" She couldn't imagine even putting them on, skirts hid legs better than any men's clothes.

"Yes, for years. I still do, honestly. There's nothing more comfortable to sleep in than a union suit."

Phoebe gasped and Will laughed.

"It's really not quite so distressing. I've been wearing one all along and no one has guessed. Keeps my ankles warm. She lifted her hems and, sure enough, instead of black wool stockings, Will had on white cotton long underwear.

"But, is it difficult…" She felt her ears turn red hot.

"Not at all, once you're used to it. The little bit of extra effort is worth the warmth. The privy is an uncomfortable place in the winter."

Hailing from Michigan, she knew this. "What else did you learn?" Phoebe leaned forward and rested her head on her palm, ready to be a pupil of this strange teacher.

"Oh, many things that aren't fit to say. When I first set out as a ranch hand, I had to learn really quickly to shut my ears at night. Men gossip almost as much as women do."

She'd never considered that. Men always seemed so aloof and unspeaking, unless they were trying to puff up like roosters. "Gossip. I suspect that's a very kind term for it."

Will shrugged, another very masculine gesture, and Phoebe cringed. "Gossip is gossip. It's all wrong. Women talk about other women and men and what's going on in everyone's lives so they don't have to think about their own. Men gossip about women and work."

Phoebe stood and joined Will at the window. Will wasn't much taller than her, nor much bigger in build. "Have you decided on a wedding date yet?"

For once, Will turned red. "I don't know. Probably spring, though that'll be busy with calves and building a herd."

"You talk about the ranching side of it, but not the marriage side. Are you worried?"

Will turned to face her and for once, she was all woman. Worry lined her face and she gripped Phoebe's arm. "Of course, I'm worried. Charles knew me as a man for a time, I know he loves me as a woman, but I don't even act like one. It's been so long. Maretta scolds me for walking the way I do, talking the way I do, even standing. I acted like a man for three years so I could fulfill my dream, but now I'm worried I'll ruin everything because I did it. Worse, part of me doesn't want to change. Won't he love me as I am?"

Phoebe extricated her arm from Will's grip then patted her shoulder. "I had no trouble telling you were a woman. But if you want me to help you, I surely will."

She half expected tears to pool in Will's eyes, but that wasn't meant to be. Instead, she frowned slightly. "I don't know what I want. If I'm to be an equal partner with Charles, then I need to know what I'm doing, but I also want him to see me as his wife." She ducked her head slightly and an unexpected giggle poured from her lips. "Kissing is quite nice."

Phoebe dropped her hand from Will's shoulder as a pain gripped her heart. She wouldn't know. She'd never let Robert kiss her. He'd wanted to, but she'd insisted they wait until the wedding. It was one more thing she'd been looking forward to, and another disappointment when he'd let her down.

"If he saw through your disguise, then I don't think you have anything to worry about. But I'm sure Maretta and I could help—if I'm still here—on your wedding day, so you can be a beautiful bride. He'll never forget that."

Will gave a half smile, but her eyes lit up. "That's a wonderful idea. I may even leave my long johns at home."

GEORGE STOOD OVER THE STOVE, cooking eggs for himself. He only ever scrambled them because they always broke anyway. It was morning and, though it wasn't his turn to cook, the man who was on the list wasn't back from whatever fun they'd had the night before.

Charles had been the only man to return to the bunkhouse and he'd already left for the morning. When George had traveled all over the South with his family, he'd never been alone. There had always been someone available, even if he just wanted to uselessly snipe at them. The other hands had all left without even asking him if he wanted to join them. He could've met them in town. The exclusion felt personal and he'd ask Kyle about it later.

If he had gone and relieved some tension, he might not be so hung up on thinking about Miss Root. She'd touched his arm, stopped him cold, made him think. *Still* made him think. But more than her touch, those deep blue eyes had formed a memory in him so real, he couldn't forget them. They made him cringe for every horrible thing he'd ever said in his past.

She was too good to be in the same room as him, so why couldn't he let her go? There was no way to get her attention without sullying her in some way. Part of him wanted to give up and shift his plan to someone else, but there just weren't any other women in Belle Fourche who made him take a second glance. His friends only talked about women they thought were pretty, so if he wanted to get the attention of a woman, he needed to feel the same. There weren't any within striking distance of Miss Root. She was one of a kind.

Charles came in and tossed his hat on the table, rushing to close the door behind him. "I can't believe Stephenia thinks this is a good time for a tour. Can't she see we're working? Not to mention it's so cold the milk cows gave icicles."

George ignored Charles' exaggeration and flipped the pan over his plate, dropping his eggs in place then set it on the warming ledge to cool off. Stephenia didn't bother with the ranch most of the time. She was the least likely member of the Oleson family to give a tour of the place. Even he knew more about it than she did. "Tour? Are there school children visiting the ranch today?" If that was so, he'd need to stay far away from her. She would make an example of him to all her students and he didn't need anyone testing him when he was plum out of niceties for the day.

"No, she's bringing around that new temporary teacher from town. I guess she moved into the house last night? Stephenia is showing her all over. I reminded her to stay away from the bull pen." Charles strode to the stove and held out his hands to warm them.

"Stephenia knows better than to go over there. She stays so far away she doesn't even usually come all the way to the barns. Arnold hitches her wagon for her every morning and everything." Not that he much cared about Stephenia, but if she was taking Miss Root for a tour, he needed to find a way to get in their way. He scooped the eggs into his mouth and swallowed, barely chewing.

"Doesn't matter. Until she's done, we can't do much. Why can't she just tell that teacher to stay up by the house?"

George dropped his empty fork onto the plate. Fastest he'd ever eaten in his life. "Her name is Miss Root and what would *you* say if Conrad told Will she couldn't go near the barns?" He paused, letting Charles think about it. "Wouldn't sit right. He's not about to tell anyone to stay away. He wants the whole family to be a part of the ranch. That's why we're allowed to stay. We're family. We're Olesons." Though he still didn't feel like he belonged. He hadn't really tried to get to know his uncle or aunt, nor his cousins, and he still waited for his uncle to pull the land away from him at any moment.

George wiped his mouth and tossed his plate into the wash bucket, then headed for the door.

"Where are you off to? Didn't you hear me? Stephenia doesn't want us around."

He laughed as he slapped his hat on. "I think it looks like a fine day for a ride." He shut the door and promised himself he'd clean up his plate when he returned. That was a bunkhouse rule. If you were the only man to dirty something, no matter if it was someone else's day for cleaning duty, you'd fix your mess. It was mighty aggravating to have one person leave untidiness everywhere, then have to clean it up before cooking. But he wouldn't be gone long enough for it to bother anyone.

Despite his prediction, it wasn't all that nice of a day. The wind whipped up around him, blowing the high grasses flat. The smoke from Uncle Nathen's chimney billowed out over the plains and George stuffed his hands into his coat pockets for warmth. While he enjoyed riding, today would not be a good day for a pleasant one.

He saddled Jerky and rode out to find Miss Root. Perhaps today he would manage to get her attention and not get tangled and tongue tied. He rode toward the house, as they might have been finishing when they'd encountered Charles. No one was near the front, so he rode around back, then down toward the east pasture. There he found Stephenia and Miss Root, standing near the fence, watching the cattle eat the last of the fall grass. The early snow hadn't killed all of the heartier grasses and once it melted, it exposed the resilient weeds.

"Good morning!" he called, pulling Jerky to a stop.

Miss Root turned around, her gray wool coat forming a perfect hourglass around her. She smiled up at him and he dismounted, just to be closer to her. He hoped she had a mind to touch his arm again and if she didn't, whatever he said would make her want to.

"Good morning, Mr. Oleson. You and your family certainly have a lot to be proud of. Your home is lovely."

He stood a little taller at her words. Compliments were rare and he'd take what he could, especially from a teacher of lofty things. "It *is* quite an impressive spread."

Stephenia turned and pursed her lips. He couldn't quite figure what he'd done to her to get her dander up, but she'd disliked him almost from the moment they'd met.

He spoke up, before Stephenia had a chance to cut him off. "Miss Root, has Mrs. Oleson shown you the foals yet? It's one of the best places on the whole ranch." John had left behind a particularly pretty foal who had the makings of a prize-winning mare, eventually. He wanted to see the look on her face when he showed her the pretty little thing.

"I'm sure I can manage to show her everything on

my own. We'd planned to have a nice walk. Alone. Good day, George."

She made him feel like one of her students and he opened his mouth to tell her just how he felt as Miss Root spoke up, holding her hand up slightly to stay his foul words.

"I would love to see it. We hadn't gotten that far yet. Stephenia had just shown me what remained of the back garden, the mums, and this fence. She told me I mustn't go inside them, though I don't see why I would want to."

He could feel Stephenia staring daggers at him, probably for not leaving the moment she told him to.

"Well, it would seem Mrs. Oleson would like to finish your tour alone. I'll leave you to it." He touched his hat, mounted his horse and lifted the reins.

"You don't have to go." Miss Root glanced up at him. "Stay. You can walk with us. It would be nice to get the perspective of someone who works here."

Stephenia gasped, her mouth falling open and eyes wide. He almost laughed, but held it in. No need to make her angrier with him.

"No, I'm sure we're fine all by ourselves. My husband was one of the *original* brothers and I can tell you all about how the ranch is run. He tells me almost everything, including who causes trouble. Saturday is the one day I have to spend as I please, I don't want to fill it correcting unruly boys like I do all week."

So, Stephenia was angry with him, at least in part, because he and his brothers had come. He wasn't one of Nathen's four sons and because they'd come, everyone's share of the land was smaller. Though it had been by choice. George and his brothers had never asked for it. Some of the land would be going back to them now that John was gone, but he'd never thought to be concerned whether Conrad, Arnold, Eli, and Barton were sore about it. They'd never acted as such.

Miss Root approached his horse and Jerky backed away, lifting his head to keep an eye on her. George patted his horse's neck.

"Is he frightened of me?" she whispered, reaching for his nose as Jerky puffed at her.

"Not frightened, just wary. He doesn't know you." George dismounted and held Jerky's bridle under his chin. "He can't smell you easily, with your coat and mittens on, is all." He patted the horse, then rubbed Jerky's favorite spot on his flank. Jerky calmed instantly and leaned in for more attention, tugging his lips into the mimic of a smile.

Miss Root laughed softly. "That is the strangest looking face I've ever witnessed a horse make. May I pet him?" When those deep blue eyes met his, he was powerless to say no.

George rubbed his hand down Jerky's muzzle, showing her how to do it. He had no idea if she'd been born in the city and didn't know, or if she was like Stephenia and had always allowed someone to do it for her, but he didn't want her to do it wrong and risk Jerky's response.

She tugged her glove off and with quivering fingers, slid her hand slowly down Jerky's forelock all the way down to his nose. Her hand stilled for a moment and her smile caught his heart and squeezed the air right from his lungs. She was prettier and more delicate than any flower, wild or otherwise.

"It's softer than I thought it would be, not the hair, but his nose. I suppose I sound foolish." She smiled softly and tugged her hand back as she ducked her head from him.

He reached for her hand and only hesitated once he realized he held it. "It's fine. You didn't sound foolish at all. Most people say it feels a little like velvet, but a horse can do some amazing things with its nose." He knew he should let her go, should release his hold, but she didn't pull away from him. He brought her hand back to Jerky and she rested her palm on the horse's forehead.

"He's a lovely horse."

Stephenia strode up to them with loud stomping steps, took Miss Root by the arm and led her off toward the barn. "I'll manage just fine from here."

He watched them walk away and realized Miss Root had done it to him again, thrown him completely off his intent. Not once had he said anything to make her blush or laugh. Nothing he could tell any of the men to make them pat him on the back. Maybe he wasn't as much of a man as he thought.

CHAPTER 4

"Stephenia, will you slow down please? You're about to tear my arm right out of the socket." Phoebe tugged free of Stephenia's surprisingly vicelike grip and rubbed the area through her coat. She'd never say so, but Stephenia's abrupt behavior had embarrassed her. Though she knew Stephenia was a little prickly because of her condition, it had gone too far.

Stephenia snorted softly. "I don't understand why that man suddenly has to come out of the woodwork and pester you every time we're outside. He didn't come to the first week you taught at the school, but now he thinks he can just come talk to you as he pleases? Simply because you're out here?" She stomped her foot. "I'll talk to Arnold about it. Obviously, George needs more work if he has all this time to pester you."

It was doubtful George needed more work, but

Stephenia had changed over the last week, grown more emotional and the smudges under her eyes bespoke of a fatigue the teacher wasn't used to. "What is the *real* problem? You don't treat any of the other townspeople with such rancor. Only him. There must be a reason." Phoebe slid her mitten back on to fend off the biting wind and stepped closer to Stephenia. She wasn't opposed to her, just confused as to why she'd taken such a strong opinion of the man. He hadn't appeared to do anything to deserve it.

Stephenia had the grace to close her eyes and grimace. "Arnold told me George was trouble, to stay clear of him for a while until he found himself. I don't know when that will happen, but I don't want to see him hurt you. He can be quite cruel, as I said."

Phoebe pursed her lips and glanced around the ranch with its sprawling fences, huge barns, various outbuildings, machinery, and men. Not a thing had bothered her on the ranch to set Stephenia off. "Didn't you also say you'd never seen him help anyone before he helped me? Maybe the change has begun? You can't keep me from getting hurt by someone else. You can only stop future growth by holding someone back who is showing progress.

"When you don't look for the change in someone, you never forgive them. You've condemned them." It would be impossible to ask George to join her class if Stephenia continued to treat him as she was. She couldn't force George to be badgered every Friday, solely so she could see if the light in his eyes was really there, or only her imagination.

"I did say that." Stephenia admitted slowly. "And I've never seen him talk to anyone as he just spoke to you. He's usually flippant and rude, which is why I choose to treat him as such."

Phoebe prayed she didn't offend her new friend by pointing out the error in her logic. "And he's said something to you, to hurt you?" If there was a real concern about him, she would make certain she was never alone with him. It would mean he was untrustworthy. Though, she suspected it was merely that Stephenia didn't know the man and was afraid to, now that her husband had bade her to stay away.

Stephenia clasped her hands together and sighed. "No, I can't say he's ever been rude to me personally and now I feel like a heel." She flushed a deep red. "Arnold told me to be wary. Perhaps I took that too far and expected him to treat me horribly. However, I *do* know he said some incredibly rude things to Will. If you want to know how George really is, talk to her. She's seen how George acts when he doesn't have to be nice."

Stephenia strode off toward her home, leaving Phoebe unsure if she should wander the ranch herself or just go back to the house and consider the tour finished. She had yet to see the foals George had claimed were the best part. Charles came out of the bunkhouse and strode toward her, flipping up his collar against the wind.

"Miss Root, good to see you. Didn't expect you to be out here all alone. I thought Stephenia was with you? Maretta probably has some tea on if you're chilly." He stopped next to her, waiting, as if he would scuttle her off at any moment.

"Thank you." She frowned, feeling like a cast-off shoe with a hole in it. "Charles, a word, if you please?"

"Sure." His gaze never left his intended target of the house and she wanted to stomp his foot to get him to look her in the eye. When she didn't budge, he finally glanced at her. "I've got a minute, but let me walk you back to the house while we talk. It's pure cold out here."

She let him walk her back and, though he'd been aggravating, she appreciated that he matched her stride. "Do you think George would ever come to a class in town?" She feared asking George outright. Many men would find that forward and perhaps it was. She didn't want to encourage any personal behavior. She'd already invited him to sign up, but he hadn't.

Charles' lips shifted to one side of his mouth. "Perhaps, if he had to. We didn't go to traditional school, Miss Root. Our sister, Natalie, taught us from books Ma had. I don't know if he would feel comfortable reading or writing with other people around. I know I wouldn't. Guess you'd have to ask him."

"Did you learn any poetry?" She prayed he'd gotten more than just the bare basics, even a taste would help. How could anyone go through school and never experience even one poem?

"Mostly just reading and writing. We learned some arithmetic, but more than that we just learned how to live. I didn't realize how much arithmetic I knew until Barton pointed out to me what I was doing when I had to figure the grain needed for winter and such. No one told me that's what I was doing, I was just solving a problem." He laughed and scratched the back of his neck. "That all, Miss Root? I really should get back to work."

"Yes, thank you." She stepped up onto the porch and glanced back over by the fence where George had been. He was nowhere in sight now. "I have five more days to convince George that poetry is no different than arithmetic."

Charles laughed as he turned away. "Don't see how you're going to manage that. I never used poetry."

That didn't mean she wouldn't try.

GEORGE SLAMMED his fist down on the table. "I don't understand what I did to Arnold's wife to make her such a mule with me."

The wrangler, Kyle, laid back in his bunk and stared at the ceiling. "Don't know. Doesn't really matter."

George shoved up from the table and put away the plate and pan he'd washed a half hour before when he'd returned from riding to find Miss Root. The task reminded him of another point of contention. "Why didn't you ask me if I wanted to join you in town? I sat here all night with nothing to do."

Kyle slid his hat over his face and crossed his arms over his chest, ignoring George's question. George stomped over and grabbed the hat as Kyle thrashed for it.

"I asked you a question. If you think you don't need to answer, I'll just toss your hat on the stove." He gripped it like a disc, ready to do just that. He hated to be ignored. Any time Pa pretended their bad behavior would just go away as they grew up, it made George even angrier and he'd behaved worse. Now it was second nature to lash out.

Kyle shot up from his bunk and scowled, taking the hat back. "Why? This is exactly why." He shook the hat in George's face. "When you don't get your way, you blow. We wanted a relaxing night at the saloon and decided to stay in town with Luke's sister. We were all in agreement we needed a night away from your schoolyard pranks and attitude." He stuffed his hat on his head. "No one wants to work with you. No one wants to spend time with you after work because your little jokes aren't funny to anyone but you. If you don't like that, only you can fix it."

Kyle strode out and slammed the door behind him. Everyone left when things got hard. Mama had said he'd reached a tough age—that he was difficult to manage—just before she got sick. Natalie had given up on him the minute she drove onto Broken Circle O land, because she didn't want his trouble anymore. Pa died without ever telling any of the boys he was proud of them and never tried to curb their ways.

He slammed the water crock down on the metal

cooktop and the hot stove cracked the pottery, shattering it all over the floor. Water sizzled and danced over the stove as George stared at the mess he'd made. He'd have to replace that, too. So many things in his life needed to be fixed or just replaced, he didn't know how to begin. It was as if the job was so large, he'd rather just bear with life as it was than face fixing it.

Charles came in, brushing off his boots on the backs of his legs and blowing air into his gloves. "What happened?" His gaze stalled on the mess all over the floor.

"I'll get a new one." He refused to say he'd slammed it down, but he wouldn't lie either.

Charles shook his head and went right to work to clean it up. Charles had always covered for George with Pa. "George. That new teacher was asking about you, wondering if you'd take a class. Maybe you should. It might give you something to think about. You've gotten hard to handle since Pa died and you won't tell anyone what's eating at you."

He didn't *tell* anyone because it was too hard to name. Anytime he even thought about Pa, it made him furious. Not sad or regretful, but angry. His father had taken something away from him, and now he'd never get it back, but he couldn't even say exactly what it was.

"I said I'd replace it. I don't need to read poetry and sit with a bunch of children." No matter how much he wanted to do just that. But there were no other men at the class that he'd heard about. Only mothers, grandmothers, and students. The men only came for the reading to watch Miss Root. A fact that burned him.

"She was concerned you might not want to come." Charles paused with the broom and dustbin in the corner then shuffled back, avoiding the shards.

"Wait?" She'd really wanted him to come? "She asked about me…specifically?" He'd assumed Charles had gotten some general invitation for all the cowboys, since so many from the other ranches were already going to the readings.

"Yes, she seemed to think you might not want to but should, or something like that. I didn't pay much attention."

George clenched his fist, then released it. Now was not the time for anger, it was a time to understand. "What, exactly, did she say?"

Charles swept up the mess and dumped it into the ash pail. "She just asked if I thought you'd ever come to her class. I said you might not because it didn't sound like anything you would do. It sounds like something you would tease the other men for doing to impress a lady."

Which was exactly why he wanted to do it, to prove Kyle wrong and to have something to talk about Friday night with the other hands. "I think I *will* go."

CHAPTER 5

Phoebe paced across the front of her classroom as Stephenia arranged the desks and chairs so more people could fit into the small building. She'd tried all week to find an excuse to go out and find George, since he'd found her twice within the first two days she'd been out there. The only time she'd come close was Sunday when they'd all attended church. However, he'd disappeared right after they'd arrived at home and she hadn't seen him since.

"If we have more people come than last week, we may have to consider doing two classes. We can't fit many more people in here." Stephenia moved things as much as possible, though the desks were bolted to the floor. She had a stack of chairs and stools to distribute throughout the room.

"As much as I hate to admit it, this week or maybe next, our numbers will drop drastically. They always do. People get busy with chores or other things. It's always interesting for them at first, a nice distraction, but if they don't really enjoy it, they stop coming." Her heart hitched slightly as it always did once she'd realized the third week was the hardest one. If no one came, she would have to leave Belle Fourche while she could and head to the next school. Her contract was only valid as long as she had students to teach and the weather kept her from leaving. The early snow had melted, allowing her to leave if there were no students.

"I'm surprised more of my pupils didn't stay after class. It may mean Millie Nickson will not join us tonight. She lives farther out of town than we do, just the next ranch over."

"She did well at her reading last week." Phoebe hated to reveal her own concern but couldn't keep from gripping her hands tight in front of her and tapping her heel as she willed the door to open.

"Don't concern yourself. I'm sure people will come." Just then, the door whooshed open, swaying her skirts. Stephenia ignored the door and kept chatting. "You're a lovely teacher. The way you read is simply moving."

"Yes, it is." A deep, sardonic voice came from a cowboy at the door, but not the one she'd been hoping for.

Phoebe stared and Stephenia turned as a cowboy from one of the Belle Fourche ranches strode in. There were too many of them from the week before for Phoebe to remember which place he came from. He had swagger and confidence. Stephenia smiled at him and offered her hand. "Jasper, good to see you again."

"Good to see you too, Mrs. Oleson." He tipped his hat then angled his gaze at Phoebe. His eyes made her skin tingle and she longed to turn away or wrap her shawl tighter around her shoulders.

"I thought there would be more people coming to your class, Miss Root. Guess I get to be your special pupil if no one else comes." He slid into a desk much too small for him and set his hat down on it with a soft *swish* that seemed to fill the room.

Phoebe concentrated on the soft noises from the wood stove to remind herself the cowboy wasn't the only thing in the room as he seemed to think. She prayed others would come but the time to start had almost arrived. She turned away from Jasper and let Stephenia keep up conversation with him. She had to concentrate on how she could manage to teach one student for two hours and then have the reading afterward.

"Good evening, ladies!" Mrs. Nickson arrived with a large pan of something that smelled like beef roast and rosemary. Millie followed her mother in and sat next to the cowboy with an impertinent smirk.

"Jasper, Mama says it's rude to ride right on by and not wave a hello." Millie notched her pert little nose in the air.

Mrs. Nickson laughed slightly and headed for the front of the room. "Shall I put this here, dear?" She headed for Stephenia's desk, which had been cleared for that purpose.

Stephenia laid down a towel to protect the wood. "That's fine. Thank you. It smells wonderful."

Just as the hour hit four, the door opened again. Phoebe held her breath as George strode in with a huge crock, covered in cheese cloth.

"I brought some warm cider. I hope that's good and there's enough." He slowly inched forward, glancing at the few people in the room.

Four students. That wasn't as many as she'd hoped, but better than none.

"That's fine, Mr. Oleson. Glad to have you here. Come in and set it down on the desk so we can begin."

THE CLASS WAS ALMOST EMPTY. George had planned to hide in a room full of students and mothers, but with only six people all together, hiding was pert-near impossible. He cut a glance at the roper who'd come in before him. He was a few years younger than George, freshly graduated last spring, but that didn't make him too young to chase after a pretty lady.

Miss Root seemed nervous, her hand quivered slightly when she stood up front. She cleared her throat often, and her cheeks were rosy, though the room was not overly warm. He'd watched Jasper for the last hour to figure out what he was doing to make Miss Root so nervous, but all he could figure was he had a look about him, because the roper hadn't said or done anything.

When they stopped to eat, Jasper rushed to the

front and scooped up a plate, then handed it to Miss Root. She again blushed and thanked him, but didn't look him in the eyes. George wanted to be there, but watching her react to Jasper made his muscles tense and sore, his jaw too, from clenching it. It was powerful hard to read poetry with a clenched jaw.

When they'd finished eating, Miss Root went back to the front and cleared her throat once more. "I'm going to come around and sit with each of you, so I can work with you especially. When I'm not with you, try memorizing the poem you choose. It will help you to read it more eloquently."

He wasn't sure what that meant, but he did know how to memorize. George ignored the noise of Millie and her mother and the halting, yet loud, reading from Jasper until Miss Root's unique musky scent wrapped around him. She touched his shoulder as she sat next to him and the light touch trickled like a warm waterfall down his arm.

"You smell like the first morning glory on a spring day after a long rainy spell." The words tumbled from his mouth before he could stop them.

Jasper broke out in great heaves of laughter. Millie sighed loudly and Mrs. Nickson made a noise somewhere between a titter and snort. Stephenia gasped and turned away. He met Miss Root's gaze and those blue eyes were soft, watery, and huge with surprise.

"Mr. Oleson, I didn't ask you to come up with your own, but that's lovely. Will you go on?"

He had to come up with more? It wasn't possible. It had been an accident. He flipped the book open so hard it slapped against the desk and Miss Root slid back from him in her chair. He lost his place and heaved a growl as he flipped through all the pages to find it again. Every solid thought he'd had flew out of his ears and he couldn't even recall the name of the poem he'd been working on.

Miss Root stood and laid her hand gently on his shoulder, stilling him immediately as he soaked in her touch. "Don't let it concern you. The reading will begin shortly. Why don't we all take a break?"

George didn't need a break, he needed to dunk his head in a bucket until he cooled off. He swiped his book from the desk and grabbed the empty crock, then headed for the door.

CHAPTER 6

The barn seemed as good a place as any to take out his frustration. Though his breath puffed above his head, George stripped to his shirtsleeves to rake out stalls and pitch hay. Since no one liked barn duty, he didn't have to worry about anyone coming to find him. No one had heard yet about what he'd said the night before to Miss Root, but it was only a matter of time. Instead of having a great story to tell after the reading, he'd left before the reading even began and avoided everyone. Two Fridays in a row he'd spent alone.

He couldn't even remember now exactly what he'd said to her, only that it wasn't manly in the slightest. She'd giggled but it hadn't been because she was impressed. It was out of genuine humor, not delight over his attention. Maybe if his father had ever taught him how to talk to a woman instead of ignoring him, he'd know better. He slammed the pitchfork into the mound of hay and growled low in his throat as barn cats scattered.

"Am I interrupting?" Miss Root's soft voice came from behind him.

He whipped around, letting the pitchfork fall with a clatter. Could he ever manage to look like anything other than a fool in front of her? "No. I was just working." He bent and grabbed the pitchfork, then stuck it into the mound so the handle was at the ready when he finished talking, which would be soon because every time he opened his mouth around her, it made a mockery of him. He crossed his arms as he waited to see why she'd come all the way out to the barn.

"Perhaps this is a bad time." Her eyes shifted from warm to wary and she backed for the door. "I'll just be on my way."

He wanted her to stay but didn't want to embarrass himself once again. "Miss Root. You don't have to go. What can I do for you? Stephenia'll have my hide if she thinks I chased you out of the barn." Which was true, but wasn't why he wanted her to stay. He still wanted to be a man, but the more he tried the more he failed. Yet, he couldn't stop thinking about her.

"But you did no such thing." Those eyes met his again and he could feel the calm on his soul the moment they met.

"It doesn't matter. That's what she'll believe."

Miss Root nodded. "So, you call her Stephenia?" The slight raise in her voice thrummed over him like he was an instrument she could play at will and with more talent than a genius.

"She's my cousin's wife. Family." There were so many Mrs. Olesons running around the ranch now, he had to call them by name or risk confusion.

"Perhaps it would be easier if you called me Phoebe, since I'm going to live here for a few months. Unless it is bothersome to you. Since we aren't family?" Though she gave the excuse, the crinkle by her eyes foretold the smile her mouth kept secret.

"Then you must call me George." His heart pounded deep in his chest. He'd never called a woman by her name, family didn't count in that way.

"It's settled then. Though, that isn't why I came out to find you."

Gooseflesh raised on his arms. She'd *looked* for him…

"You found me. What is it you need?" He had to test her name on his lips, couldn't stop himself. "Phoebe."

She smiled and hid her hands behind her back as she tucked her chin. "You left last night. Angry. I didn't mean to embarrass you. I was so impressed by what you'd said, I couldn't stop thinking about it."

She'd remembered what he'd said without thinking? Without planning and posturing?

"Who did you write it for? May I see or even just hear the rest of it? Please? It's so rare that I find anyone who wants to do more than read poetry others have written."

He rubbed his forehead. There was no way out but a straight shot. "I didn't write it. I just said it."

"Oh." Her eyes grew wide as her brows shot up.

"It's not that I didn't mean what I said at the time. I mean, every time you get anywhere near me it's like I can't be myself no matter how hard I try." Like right now, when his head screamed for him to leave before he said anything more foolish. But where Phoebe was concerned, his heart was in control and it wasn't listening to reason.

"You…meant it. For me?" She tilted her head and tried to look him in the eye.

He'd always considered himself a straight shooter, but admitting his heart had more control over his mouth than he did, even for a little while, didn't make him feel like one. "Yes, you. I wasn't talking about Millie," he grumbled.

She laughed and took a few steps closer. "I'm so glad. I was worried you'd left because I'd put you on the spot. I am sorry… And thank you. Your compliment was the most beautiful thing anyone has ever said to me. I wrote it down after you left, before the reading, so I wouldn't ever forget."

He grabbed his coat, suddenly chilled. Nothing was going to plan. He couldn't tell the men in the bunkhouse he'd made her pleased as punch about some frothy words. They would laugh at him. And the more he considered what to do next, the more he wanted Phoebe's attention to matter, more than just gaining her attention because he was a man, but because he wanted to be *her* man.

"All is forgiven?" She stepped even closer and the words he'd forgotten about morning glories and rain flooded back over him. Her scent was perfect.

"Nothing to forgive." He tried to take a deep breath, but the beating of his heart wouldn't let him.

"Will you show me the foals? Stephenia never got around to it." She stood next to him now, and her temple was just the height of his shoulder. Was there anything about her he could find amiss? If he didn't discover something soon, he'd find himself trying to court a teacher and there were already three Mrs. Oleson's who'd trained as teachers.

IT SEEMED as natural as rain to reach out and link her arm with George's as he walked her to the foal barn. She'd never been on a ranch so big the foals needed a special barn. Though, when they arrived, she saw why he'd said it was so special. It was very small and odd. The building itself was a dome shape, with triangular pieces built together and tilted so it formed a circular building with a rounded roof.

"I was told Uncle Nathen drew up the plans for this building while Maretta was having Conrad, her firstborn. The story goes that Uncle Nathen was kept away for two days while she labored."

Phoebe had no doubt, Conrad was a big fellow. She leaned in closer and George smiled as her shoulder brushed against his. "When it was all done, the doctor came out and pronounced him a father, then took one look at the drawing and laughed. Said he'd never build such a thing. Nathen told him if his wife could make a baby in nine months, he'd make that building in four. And he did. It's been standing here ever since."

Phoebe laughed, but her heart ached too. The mention of a baby was again tugging on her. "What is it about men? Always trying to do one better? Wasn't he proud of the baby? His wife had just spent two days to give him a son."

"Of course he was, still is. Nathen is a great father."

She sensed he wanted to say more, but hesitated to push him. Sometimes, it felt like she'd known him since before time existed. Others, like then, she knew nothing about him. "I can only assume. He has built a wonderful, strong family."

George seemed placated by her response and led her into the small dome. The ceiling was low, which kept it warmer inside. There were four pens, each large enough for a foal and a mare, though all the foals were now alone.

"Aren't they still with their mothers?" Though she knew little about horses, she'd thought they nursed for at least a year and it was only late fall.

"They do, but you can't keep the mares penned up all day. Each pen has a gate that we raise to let her in or let them out. The gate leads out to one big fence. They can be taken from there anywhere else out the side gate. Come see this one." He took her hand and led her to the pen in the back right. Inside, was a red foal with black stockings. Her eyes were bright and alert, and she seemed ready to jump as if she had too much energy for the small pen.

George reached in and it steadily walked up and snorted over his hand, puffing deeply.

"Her name is Stormy. She was supposed to be my brother, John's. He left her behind and I want to ask Uncle Nathen if I can buy her."

She touched George's hand where it was braced against the pen and he dropped his attention from the foal immediately and stared at it. "Why would he give the foal to John, but make you buy it?"

George gave a slight shrug and stared back into the pen. The foal would come no closer and looked on Phoebe with eyes that suspected threat.

"Horses never like me," she said, trying not to let the foal's rejection bother her. "It seems they know I can't help them, nor can I do anything for them. I'm a burden, and somehow they're smart enough to know it."

"Horses *are* smart, but I doubt they think any such thing about you. They can tell when you're afraid. Are you afraid?"

That question was fraught with the danger of twenty blizzards. She feared so many things, the least of which were the horses. If that sweet little beast sensed anything in her it wasn't fear of the horse itself. More like terror over what would happen to her if she didn't schedule more schools. Fear over where she would live if she had to find a home. She'd never be able to teach general studies, and didn't hold the qualifications to do so.

"Phoebe?" George's voice rattled her from the stronghold of her thoughts.

"I'm sorry. Yes, George, I am afraid. I only have one more school scheduled after Belle Fourche and it's only for three weeks. After that, I'm not sure what I'll do."

"There's always a way, if it's the path you're supposed to be on."

Her heart yearned for the assurance she'd had when she started on the journey. There would always be schools, more students, more lives. The deeper into the West she got, the more distant that assurance became. People of the West were already self-assured and while they enjoyed listening to others read poetry as some would like to go to a play, they had no interest in trying their own hand.

"My art is dying." And as she spoke it aloud, she knew it in her heart to be true. Time never stood still.

"Not while you love to do it and continue to do it." George reached over and squeezed her hand, but she couldn't look at him. He was so strong and capable. He would always have a place, something to do where he would fit in. Yet, he hadn't acted like all of the other men. He'd been humble and quiet. The mocker had disappeared in her presence.

"I do love it, but I can only love so much until the love will wear me thin. Then what will I do?"

He smiled and released her hand. "You'll find a way to love some more. That's what you do when your dream becomes your life." He tipped his hat and left her with the little foals in the odd-shaped barn.

Could love sustain her, or did it take more than that to survive?

CHAPTER 7

George took a deep breath as he yanked on his boots. Charles lingered over him like a mother hen.

"Just what do you think you're doing? It's not your job to teach anyone how to ride. Eli's the one who breaks horses, best leave it to him to teach her if she wants to learn."

George gritted his teeth and held in what he wanted to say to his overly-concerned brother. "What are you so afraid of, Charles? Are you worried I'll get us into trouble, yet again? Are you worried I'll live up to my reputation and scare her right off the place?" George shot to his feet ready to duke it out with his older brother. He was only older by two years, not enough of a difference to matter.

"Cool your heels, George. I don't think anything of the sort."

"All of you do. Why is it that John was allowed to

change, started acting like he was supposed to, and everyone believed it, took his word that he was a good man. The same for you. You were given the task of watching over Will to test you, and sure enough, everyone saw that you were a man who could do the right thing. But when it comes to me, everyone, and I mean *everyone*, acts like I'm going to chase Phoebe around with skunk spray and call her a heifer."

"I recommend butter." Barton stood from his seat at the table and leaned against it. If his face hadn't been utterly serious, George would've assumed he was trying to poke fun at him.

Charles laughed humorlessly as he glanced back and forth between George and Barton, his hands out at his sides, ready to stop a fight.

Barton chuckled slightly. "Before I courted Lula, before I even knew courting was what I wanted to do, I pestered her awfully. I was downright mean. One time, when the well was running low at the Spearfish Normal School, and I knew she couldn't wash her hair, I caught her and slathered butter in those lovely curls of hers. Once I figured out that woman was meant to be mine and I'd made a life of mistakes, I had to make it right. Sometimes, it takes manning up for a long time for people to see you differently."

Barton took a deep breath and flexed his fingers over the chair rail. "It took months, with human imperfections and failures, for me to convince Lula I was not only sorry for what I'd done to her, but that I was man enough for her to trust me."

"Well, that's very interesting. But at the school, you

didn't have everyone reminding you of your past every time you opened your mouth." Though it wasn't that bad, with Stephenia and the hands reminding him every chance they got, it sure felt like it.

"No, I didn't, but are you ready to hear how you start or do you want to keep fighting with me?" Barton stared him straight in the eyes. "I'm trying to get through to you that there is hope, a way out. You don't have to be the mean cuss people think you are."

"I'm listening." He had to stop opening his mouth every time someone spoke to him. Wasn't that exactly how he'd stuck his foot in it last night with Miss Root?

"The first thing you do is stop living for a reaction, and start living with a focus on what is right. Then trust and respect will follow. Not just right in her eyes, but God's."

Charles nodded slightly. "It's true. When I stopped trying to impress Pa, because he wouldn't see me anymore anyway, and started trying to just do what was right so I could have the respect of Uncle Nathen, then I gained the respect of all the hands."

It sounded so easy, but George knew it wasn't. He'd already been doing the work of a man, so he'd thought acting like a man meant participating in the bunkhouse talk of women, cards, and work after the lamps had been snuffed. Though he could honestly say the men who joined in didn't have his respect, nor were they honorable. He'd been looking at it all wrong.

"I'm going to teach her how to ride. You'll have to trust me."

Barton patted him on the shoulder. "That's a good start. Just remember who you are."

He left the bunkhouse and made his way to the house. Since it was Tuesday, Stephenia wouldn't be there to warn Phoebe away from him. That particular Mrs. Oleson would be the most difficult to get through to, since she'd already pegged him as trouble forever.

He knocked on the door and Will answered. He'd seen her around and it still shocked him to see her in a dress. Though he knew she was a woman and she'd only acted as a man, women were supposed to be frail and soft, Will was not.

"Good morning, George. What can I do for you?"

Was Will preventing him from going into his own uncle's house? "You can let me in, for starters."

Will frowned and backed away from the door, ushering him in. He brushed past her and headed for the kitchen. That's where the only noise in the house came from and it seemed the most plausible place to find Phoebe. He pushed through the door and found Aunt Maretta on a stool dusting the top of a cabinet with Phoebe holding her legs.

"Land sakes, boy! Don't you knock?" Maretta lost her balance for a moment and gripped the cabinet.

He lurched forward to catch her if she fell and bumped into Phoebe. She gasped and reached for Maretta to make sure she didn't tumble.

"Well, now that I've got everyone at my feet I can get this done without any worry at all." Maretta scowled, finished swiping the rag over the top of the cabinet, then gripped his shoulder tightly to climb down. "There. Now what is it you want, George?"

Maretta often treated him as if he was a nuisance, but in her defense, he had been. "I wanted to come in and offer Phoebe a riding lesson. Since she's teaching me a new skill, it's only fair I teach her one as well."

Maretta smiled and glanced between the two of them. "Yes, yes, that's fine." She took Phoebe by the shoulders and stood her next to George. "Hmm, well, I have no say in the matter, but you both are a little young. Well, at least you are, Phoebe dear. George is twenty-three. Same as his brother Charles, just three months apart. Isn't that right, George?"

Barton had said doing what was right would be hard, but he hadn't thought he'd be confronted with the one time he'd lied right to his uncle and aunt's faces. "Twenty-one, ma'am. I was worried Uncle Nathen might not give me any land if I was too young. Now I know I acted too young anyway."

Maretta smiled and pushed Phoebe just a bit closer. "I know, dear. Your sister told me. And, I think I was wrong. You two look just fine."

HIS SHOULDER BUNCHED next to hers and Phoebe had the strangest urge to reach over and feel it under her fingertips, not just through all her layers of clothing to her arm. Her palms were damp against her clenched fingers as she glanced at George. Not only would she be with him all afternoon, but on a horse. She'd never been allowed to ride.

Maretta went back to her dusting and Phoebe leaned closer to him, felt the heat of his face, and breathed in the scent of his shaving soap. Her mind lingered in the moment, hunting for the perfect words to describe what she felt and came up empty. What kind of poet lost her words at the scent of a man? Shouldn't such a wonderful thing fill her senses and excite her vocabulary?

"Are you certain this is a good idea? Horses don't like me." Though she'd never really given them a chance.

"They will learn." His voice was lower than normal, full of tension and deeper meaning than she could fathom.

"Then I'll get my things." She headed for the kitchen coat tree where she'd left her coat, muffler, and gloves when she'd returned the day before from walking outside and visiting the foals. Never had she dreamed she'd try to ride the very next day. "Am I dressed properly?" She slid on her coat, then turned and held her arms out for his inspection. Though she'd seen women riding before, she hadn't at the Broken Circle O. Did they have what she would need?

"You're perfect." He held out his hand and her heart begged her to wait, savor the moment, recall every sensation because the next school would call her away and her time with George would be fleeting. She'd never felt her heart plummet and jolt so, and doubted it would again soon.

"Perfect," she scoffed as she tugged on the wool cap Maretta had told her to wear. She felt silly in it, but it was much warmer than any bonnet or women's hat.

Instead of answering, George took her hand and led her out the back door. Without saying another word, he directed her back to the paddock where two horses waited. One was his horse and she thought she recalled him calling it, Jerky. The other she'd not seen.

"You've already met Jerky, but this is Mule. She's a sweet old girl. Perfect for someone to learn on."

She wanted to ask about the strange names of the horses, but then she would have to wait longer to ride.

"First." George turned to face her and looked her right in the eyes. His gaze didn't travel down as some men's did, nor did he pretend to pay attention, humoring her. He was all business and it calmed her quaking nerves. She met his stare and listened. "I need you to listen to what I say. Always watch the horse, until you learn to ride well enough that you can tell what it will do, then *really* watch the horse, because it will think it's pulled one over on you."

She laughed and it made him smile and his eyes brightened. When he didn't smile, he had the appearance of constant anger or an aloof nature that was not welcoming. But when he did, his attractiveness couldn't be denied. His sandy hair just brushed his ears below his hat and begged her fingers to push it out of the way. Her heart pounded and she averted her eyes, hoping he didn't notice her overlong concentration.

"Most women ride side-saddle, but I've never taught anyone how to ride aside, and I couldn't find an aside saddle in the tack room, so we'll have to be as careful as possible when you mount and dismount."

She felt heat rush up her face. "Perhaps I should've borrowed Will's long johns."

A brief look of disgust washed over George's face and she saw a window into the man he'd been hiding from her. No man was perfect. She quickly tried to return him to good humor. "I'm sure I'll be fine. You shouldn't see any more than my boots with all the petticoats I have on to keep warm."

He nodded, but she'd felt a chill slip between them. She'd have to find out what ill-will he held against Wilhelmina. If she was to become Charles' wife, it would only sew strife in the family.

"Always mount from the left" He turned to face the horse and held the stirrup for her.

"Why?" She'd always seen it done that way and had no idea what the purpose was or why it should matter.

"Because many people who ride, also ride armed. The scabbard for a long rifle is on the right making it easier to grab on to. So, we mount from the left." He waited for her to step forward, but her nerves weren't ready for getting on the horse just yet. No matter how gentle Mule looked.

"But I'm not shooting. Does it really matter?"

He straightened his spine and fixed his gaze on the saddle for a moment, then sighed. "What was the first thing I asked you to do?" He scratched his forehead without looking at her. He was frustrated with her, but still not treating her the way Stephenia had said he would. She smiled and stepped forward, taking his hand. "You said to listen to you."

His eyes lightened and it brightened his whole face. "Now that you can do that, are you ready to trust me?"

In that moment, she knew she could. "Yes, I believe I am."

CHAPTER 8

George rode alongside Phoebe and did his best to keep his eyes from roaming to her boots. He was certain he'd never seen feet so small. Were all women's feet that small, or just hers? Men's boots didn't fit like women's boots. Women's footwear hugged their feet tightly up the calf and continued under the hems of her skirt. He'd never seen a woman with bare feet, so he'd never noticed how tall women's boots were, covered beneath all that fabric.

He led the horses down to a path he'd found when he'd been out riding early on, when he'd first come to the ranch and had wanted to get away from his cousins. They had all tried to whip him into something he hadn't been ready for then. Now, he was glad of it. He hadn't been back down the lonely, low path in a long time, but it was out of the wind and an easy ride for Phoebe.

"Are you taking me somewhere in particular?" Only then did he notice her eyes were wider than usual, and she gripped the reins as if Mule might buck her off at any moment.

He'd been so focused on the trail and on her feet that he'd forgotten to talk to her, reassure and calm her. "Not a destination as much as I wanted to follow this trail. It's out of the wind. Peaceful. You can hear your thoughts and the horse can't run on you easily, because of the hills on each side." He cut a glance at her and waited for her response.

"It is." She shivered.

"Are you cold?" He'd been used to living his life outside, so being uncomfortable was simply a part of who he was. He'd thought getting her out of the wind would be enough.

"Can we stop for just a little while?" Her teeth chattered.

He tugged the reins and Jerky stopped short, hating the feel of the halter when it was taught. Mule didn't even need a cue, she just stopped when Jerky did. He dismounted and Miss Root watched his hands with wide-eyed trepidation as he reached up to help her down.

"I think I can manage, if you tell me how to do it." She held the reins in her hand exactly as he'd shown her when they set out, except they were so loose, Mule wouldn't have even known she'd held them at all.

"Wrap the reins around the pommel, then stand in the stirrups."

She raised an eyebrow at him. "Won't the horse get angry with me and jolt me right off when I have nothing to hold on to?"

He laughed at the idea of Mule doing anything in a hurry. She didn't even hurry to the feed trough. "Remember, rule one."

Phoebe pursed her lips, turning them a dark pink in the cold. He couldn't stop his gaze from lingering on them, bright against her pale skin. Even her rosy cheeks seemed faint compared to the bow of her lips.

"Yes, yes. Trust you." She put the reins together and laid them over the saddle, then stood slowly, holding tight to each side.

"Now lift your right leg over the horse, swing it over, and lower yourself to the ground."

She did just as he'd told her and his heart pounded and muscles tensed as he imagined her falling backward and landing right in his arms. She would thank him then and probably give him a kiss just for his trouble.

"George? Whatever are you smiling about?" Phoebe laughed, bringing his attention back and his heart sank as he realized she was already safe with feet planted on the ground. "Did I look quite that silly?"

He forced the smile off his face. "No, not at all. I'm just glad you made it down on your first try. You're doing wonderful." Now if he could manage to do the same. She'd taken on something new and done just fine, now it was his turn.

"You would think I'd be used to cold. Michigan

isn't warm in the winter." Her teeth rattled together and he reached up and tugged the knit cap lower over her ears to cover them better. He hated concealing that pretty red hair, but he didn't want to see her get sick.

"I never went through Michigan. When we came to Belle Fourche, we drove through Kansas, then Nebraska, headed North to Belle Fourche. What's it like there?" He wanted to make her think about something other than being cold as he took her hands and rubbed them.

She watched his hands intently and allowed him to continue. Her tongue darted out of her mouth and licked her lips as she leaned slightly toward him. He side-stepped so she was between himself and the horse to block any wind, though he couldn't feel any.

"It's green." She laughed, but he knew it wasn't green there all the time, she was trying to remember warmth, maybe family sitting around a fire...

"And did you leave family behind to travel all over, teaching students about poetry and judging contests?" He wanted to tug off her gloves and feel her skin against his own. Her hands would be much softer even than the leather kid gloves she wore. They were useless out on a ranch, but for a teacher, perhaps they were fine.

"Family." Her eyes closed softly. "I wish it were true."

He held her hands tighter to give her what comfort he could. If he were as much a man as he wanted to be, he'd have pulled her close and held her, but he wasn't. Hadn't he proven that? He'd been such a buffoon around her. "Before we came to South Dakota, I thought all I had were my sister and brothers."

The ghost of a smile touched her lips and she opened her eyes. "Then you have much."

"I do. What can I give to you?" He cringed inside. How could he keep opening his mouth without any thought where this woman was concerned?

She laughed and tugged her hands from his. "Nothing. You've given me enough by joining my class. It's rare I meet anyone who actually takes an interest in poetry and even more rare to meet anyone with a gift."

He wanted to laugh, to admit the truth. He didn't have a lick of interest in poetry. Only in her. He found her reading jarred something within him, but nothing from anyone else, and if he truly had a gift, wouldn't he want to hear it from anyone? Or create his own? "You think I have a gift? I assure you, I don't, unless that gift is opening my mouth when it should remain shut."

"No, that's not so. It can't be. You've done so well, and I saw it in you that first time you came." She flinched and rubbed her hands together. "I think we need to go back. I've seen enough."

Seen? Or heard? George wished again he'd simply kept quiet. He reached for her back to keep her from falling, but she swung into the saddle easily. He caught up Jerky's reins and mounted, feeling less like he should say anything.

Phoebe was lonely, and worried. That's why she was agreeable to see him. She'd been looking for a friend to pass the time and he was available. Hadn't she said she had nowhere to go after her next school? With no place to teach and no family to return to, where *would* she go? He shouldn't concern himself with her, but that didn't stop him. Her teeth began to chatter once again and that set a new crop of worry in him. What if his riding lesson made her sick? It wasn't even winter yet and she was mighty chilled for the late fall weather.

"I'll get you back to Aunt Maretta's. We don't have to ride anymore."

He heard a slight sniffle. "I'm sure I'll be ready for another lesson once it warms up. I don't think I learned much. I forgot to even pick the reins back up and Mule just followed you."

He glanced back and, sure enough, the reins trailed on the ground and Phoebe sat in the saddle, holding onto the pommel and staring at the ground in front of her. He slowed and caught Mule's halter, then gathered the reins. He tried to hand them to Phoebe but she shook her head.

"You take them. You're better at this than I am." She tucked her chin to her chest and her shoulders hunched, making her appear slight on the large horse.

He remembered Barton's advice, to stop trying to get attention and just do what was right. It would be more than twenty minutes until they made it back to the house and he couldn't leave her in the saddle, cold and shivering. He unbuttoned his coat and peeled it off, handing it to her. "Here, put it on. It's too far back to the house for you to wait."

"But, I can't do that." She shook her head and Mule halted, almost unseating her. "You'll freeze out here."

While he could appreciate her concern, it wasn't warranted. "Take it. Put it on. I'll be fine until we get back. When we do, get in the house and by the stove. Warm up right away."

Though he'd spent plenty of time trying to order the men in the bunkhouse to do what he thought they should, it didn't sit well to order Phoebe to do something, even something for her own good. He didn't need the coat, he'd worn layers as he usually did and though it wasn't comfortable, she needed it more. She tentatively wrapped it around her, then stuck her arms through and huddled in. He was average size for a man, but even with her own winter clothes on, his coat still sat huge over her narrow shoulders.

She held out her hands, completely covered by his sleeves. "I guess you'll have to take the reins now."

He thought about that and smiled. Yes, he would take the reins, because it didn't matter what men said to each other over a deck of cards. That didn't make him who he was. It was what he did with the reins once they were in his hands that mattered. Maybe it wasn't about ordering men around, either. It was about just doing the work no matter whose job it was. That way, he could hold his tongue and be known as a man who got things done. What he'd planned as a ride to teach Phoebe, had opened his own eyes.

A dainty sneeze from behind him caught him off-guard and he flinched. Maybe he'd gained a lot from the ride, but all she'd gained was a cold. "Don't worry, Phoebe, we'll get you home quick."

CHAPTER 9

Even the barn wasn't warm as George led Mule inside and Phoebe huddled deeper within George's warm ranch coat. As soon as they halted, she dismounted and waited for George to take it back. He slid off Jerky and stared at her for a second as heat roiled up her neck. She had to look foolish in the wool knit cap tugged down to her neck —even covering her down to her eyes—and his giant coat. She glanced down at herself, drowning in the wool-lined, canvas mackinaw. But it was very warm and when she tucked her chin inside the collar, she could smell his shaving soap.

"You need to go on into the house. Warm up. Your blood isn't ready for South Dakota yet."

She chuckled, but felt fine now that she had his warmth surrounding her. "I'd better get used to it. I can't leave until April. Dr. Spight said the trains start running regular again about that time."

He nodded, but he'd gone right to work removing Mule's saddle. Though he'd told her to listen to his rules, especially rule number one, he couldn't make her go into the house and she wasn't quite ready to leave him behind yet. His question about family had made her think deeply about what she would do in June, when she had nowhere to go. Her family was not expecting her return because they had been angry she hadn't chosen to continue the family business. His flippant remark about poetry had also made her think. Had she missed the signs once again? Was he lying to her?

"What would you have done if you weren't a cowboy?"

He chuckled and slipped the saddle off the horse's back. "I don't know. My father used to make limbs for amputees before he died, but he didn't teach my brothers and I how to do that. I guess we were lucky Uncle Nathen took us in and his sons taught us how things are done." He eyed her and a half-smile crept over his face. "You going to stay out here, or go inside?"

She wanted to linger, to thank him for his time and bothering with her. So many people seemed to think she only existed on Fridays when she was at the school. They went about their lives every other day and thought of her as only the extra teacher. George had taken the time to remember her and she wouldn't soon forget that.

She reached for the collar of the coat to peel it off and he held up his hand for her to stop. "Don't. If you take it off now, you'll get extra cold. Just take it with you in the house and hang it up by the back door. I'll come get it when I'm done."

"And will you come see me?" She bit her lip against the roiling in her stomach. She'd never been so bold before. But she'd never met a man like George before, either. So honest and good, at least, she was certain of that much. He had been good to her in every way, from taking her trunk into the house, showing her the foals, taking her for a ride, and even giving up his coat. She couldn't forget those things when Stephenia or anyone else spoke up against him.

He tipped his chin a bit to hide his own smile. "I'll come and check on you when I get my coat. Go on, now, and warm up."

She turned and picked her way out of the barn past hay and other obstructions. It wouldn't take George long to finish with Jerky and he would come to the house to find her soon, though it had looked like he'd been wearing enough clothes to keep him warm. He hadn't seemed cold at all compared to her. She sniffled again as the wind bit at her nose.

She pulled open the door and the warm kitchen was a welcome retreat with the smell of a fresh-baked loaf of bread lingering near the door. The large cookstove along the back wall beckoned to her and she slid off George's coat, then her own before she pulled up a stool and warmed her hands in front of the blackened metal.

George had brought up two things on their ride that she'd been loath to think about, but had to, soon.

The first was, without another school to go to in June, she would be without a job. The second was, she had no family to fall back on and the reason for that could be repeating itself. George could be just like Robert. She'd let Robert into her heart too, though he'd never made her feel so excited.

Her family had celebrated her match with Robert. They had given parties and planned a large wedding. Robert was going to take over the family lumber business, and support her in her endeavor to start a poetry school. About a week before the wedding, Robert drank too much at one of the many parties they attended and tried to lead her to a back room. When she wouldn't go with him, he'd shown his true colors and told her he didn't care about her, only her family's lucrative business. Her mother had suggested they just ignore the behavior, since he'd been inebriated and Father already liked Robert. They both thought he was a good fit for the company. She'd spent a week contacting benefactors, and the moment she'd found one willing to take her on, she'd left to become a traveling teacher.

And had never looked back.

There were no other towns she'd been to where she could return and stay. No friends who would take her in. Other years, she'd traveled to Texas, Alabama, or Florida during the fall and stayed all winter, going from school to school until the spring. Then she could go anywhere she wished again. When Belle Fourche had requested she come, they had offered to pay her salary for the entire winter, which had been generous, but also made it difficult to plan ahead.

The next school she would attend wasn't even far away, but it was the only school willing to book her service so far in advance. The Spearfish Normal School was only a few hours away by train, and only needed her for a few weeks at the very end of their term before graduation. They already studied poetry and had asked her to come as a judge for a contest instead of as a teacher. Her employer hadn't sent her any letters since her arrival, nor had he sent her the share of the pay she was due. Usually, she would've received it already. Without that, she truly had no options left. If she didn't hear from Mr. Fairchild before spring, she wouldn't even have the money to go to the next school.

Anne Oleson came in from outside and smiled at her. "Miss Root, good to see you. Have you been outside or are you sitting too close to the stove? Your cheeks are so rosy."

She hadn't felt her best since the reading when George had left, and after being outside riding, it had gotten worse. At the reading, there had been an infant who'd been crying, fussy, with ruddy cheeks and an inconsolable cry. She'd held the baby while her mother helped her other two children sit down. Phoebe had enjoyed holding the little one so much, she kept it through most of the reading, rocking and bouncing the child to keep it quiet.

"I took a riding lesson from George. I daresay, it's

chillier here than I thought it would be, and earlier than I thought as well."

Anne nodded, but her gray eyes narrowed slightly. "A riding lesson with George?"

Did everyone think so little of him? She had seen almost no hint of this aggression everyone seemed to think was part of his nature. Had he pulled the wool over her eyes, or was he just different with her? "Yes, he decided if I was going to be on a ranch all winter, I should know how to ride, or at least how to be led on a horse." She laughed and rubbed her hands together. It felt so strange to be defending a man.

"Well, I do agree with him. Which is a first, I might add." Anne pulled up another stool and sat next to her, though she didn't try to warm herself. "I'm glad I caught you. I had hoped to come to the reading last week, but had a late arrival at the clinic. I hope to come this week. I don't want you to think the doctor and I aren't supportive."

She hadn't thought any such thing. The only doctor and nurse within many miles were probably busier than bees in the summer. She hadn't thought they would come at all. "Think nothing of it. If you come, I'll be pleased. If you don't, I'll assume you were too busy."

"I've never been one to read much poetry, but I do love to listen to it. Now Isabelle, she loves poetry. Wordsworth is her favorite."

"Yes, I've talked with her about that, but she can't come to the readings because she likes to watch Conrad play with Junior on the floor in the evening."

Phoebe's heart did a little flip as it often did when she thought of babies, but even more when she thought of great strong men holding them. There was something about a man holding a wee being that made a woman ready to have her own ache all the more.

Anne nodded slightly. "Yes, those two love that child, but it's because Isabelle wasn't sure she'd be able to conceive at all. He's a special blessing to them."

What would it be like to go through what Abraham's wife Sarah had in Genesis? To go from barren to having a son? Phoebe bit her lip and held it. She would be barren, not because she couldn't have children, but because there would be no one for her if she continued to travel.

There would never be a baby for her arms or a loving husband to play with it on the floor. She would never have a home or fire. But if she gave up teaching, abandoned her post, the love of poetry would come one step closer to its death. Her benefactor had been so passionate about it, so sure she had to go out and be the missionary for the cause. But what of her own heart?

"A child would be a blessing. I can only imagine. Stephenia tells me she, too, may be expecting a little one in the spring."

Anne nodded, a soft smile lighting her eyes. "Yes, it's true. The only Oleson brother who will be childless is Eli." Her eyes turned glassy and she stood, turning away from Phoebe. She gripped her hands in front of her and her shoulders tightened.

"I'm sorry, Anne. I didn't mean to bring up

anything to hurt you."

"We've told the family that the house is too small for children, but, well, you mustn't tell the others. Eli and I have managed to get with child twice, but lost it both times. I…" Her voice cracked and her shoulders shuddered.

Phoebe stood and wrapped what she hoped was a comforting arm around Anne, having some small idea of how she felt without ever going through just the same thing. No one would comfort a healer, because the healer would never tell others of her ailments, just like no one thought of the teacher when it wasn't a school day.

"I pray that you will be blessed with life, Anne. I pray that you will not have to wait any longer."

Anne turned into the embrace and cried softly on Phoebe's shoulder. She'd never felt a part of a family, not close or personal, had never had friends to talk to. This was exactly what she would've been giving up if she had ignored Robert's behavior and married him. No one would ever have comforted her.

"Please, keep praying for me, but His will be done. If we are meant to be without children, we are still happy to have each other." Anne rose from her shoulder and wiped her eyes.

"I will. Don't lose heart."

Was there someone out there who would be that for her? The one who, no matter what the Lord willed for either of their lives, would always be by her side? Had her choice to be a spinster forced a man to be alone, too?

George pushed through the door and Anne quickly left to find Maretta. He stood by the entrance for a moment, his face flush with cold and his hair windblown. His eyes were the deepest blue as they took her in and neither spoke.

George was alone and she'd felt drawn to him almost from the beginning. Was he the man who would have no one if she chose to remain a spinster? He was a man in a town where women were rare. If she left, he might never find anyone else. Could she face the knowledge that her choice condemned a man to loneliness?

He collected his coat, but didn't move to put it on right away. How did so many people think ill of him, when he'd treated her so well? He stepped forward and lifted the hat slowly off her head. She'd been in such a hurry to sit by the warm fire, she'd forgotten it was even there. Loose pins fell to the floor and some of her hair tumbled down her back. George stood staring at it for a minute and her stomach fluttered as he reached for a single hank. He picked up one lock and tucked it behind her ear.

"That's the reddest hair I've ever seen."

She'd hated it. All the catalogues in the stores featured women with brown hair, to frame a beautiful face. No one wanted to be a redhead, with her smattering of freckles in the summer and skin far too fair. Not creamy, like others, but almost ashen to her own eyes. She took up the hair that had fallen and tried to stick it into the remaining pins, all with the hope she didn't look as unkempt as she felt.

"Don't." He lightly held her arm, then brought it down. He reached up again and gently tugged a pin loose, causing more hair to fall. "It's like sunshine on fall leaves." He closed his eyes as he released her hair, handing her the pin. "I'm sorry. I shouldn't have."

Her body trembled and knees went limp. She reached for him, wanted him to stay, to prove that he felt that pull to her and it wasn't all in her imagination.

He had to understand her. Only a fellow poet could.

As her hand touched his arm he stretched his around her, pulling her flush against him. His lips were full and eyes hot as they traveled over her face. Did she dare allow herself to stay in his embrace, no matter how much she wanted it? She would leave and could get a new assignment soon, then another, and before she could blink, Belle Fourche would be her distant past. The future was too confusing to allow herself to add to it by falling for George.

His lips brushed hers and she let out a small cry. The kiss should've been expected, but she'd been too lost in thought to realize what had happened until it was done. Yet he didn't pull away completely.

"Your scent is like a morning glory after a rain. Your hair like sun on fall leaves. I cannot get enough. Your lips are soft as spun candy and twice as sweet. I cannot stop myself from tasting again." He tugged her close, pressed his lips to hers and this time, she didn't worry about the future, the past, or even the present as a loud gasp came from the door behind him.

CHAPTER 10

The church had been less full than normal and George tried briefly to figure out if he knew any of those missing, but he was simply too preoccupied with glancing down the row at Phoebe to concentrate on anything else for long. She wore a blue shirt that exactly matched her eyes and it had been so striking he hadn't been able to think well enough to speak when he'd seen her.

She had blushed that morning when he'd come in to offer his arm to walk her out to the wagon. He'd even brought a thick, wool blanket for her for the ride. She'd allowed him to fuss over her, but had said nary a word. While Charles encouraged him to continue to get Phoebe's attention, all the other Olesons seemed to staunchly disapprove. Especially Stephenia, who had loudly pronounced he needed to beg forgiveness for his boorish behavior.

Though Stephenia was only looking out for

Phoebe, he'd felt like he shouldn't say anything more, and had kept to himself since. They all arrived back after service and all the women took the children inside for naps and to prepare a late lunch. Barton followed George into the barn to unhitch the team.

"Anne told Eli you got caught in the kitchen with Miss Root," Barton said as he unhooked the traces and gathered the lines.

He'd been pulled in by the color of her hair, her smile, her soft voice, the scent of the outdoors wrapped around her. Even now, he wanted to be in the house where she was and she'd wanted him, too. He'd felt a connection grow between them when he'd kissed her. "It isn't like I buttered her hair."

"Didn't you? Some men are glib with affection. They don't think kisses mean much and maybe to some men, they don't. I know they can lead a man to a dangerous place. A hard decision. Just make sure you're still doing what's right and not looking for that reaction."

George had been searching for a reaction, but only for himself. Not from the other men, and in fairness, not from her. Maybe he had buttered her hair in a manner, because he'd done it without really thinking about if they would have a future. He'd only thought about that moment and how much he'd wanted her close, so close he could taste her.

"Do you remember your parents?" Barton finished unhitching one of the two wagons they'd taken.

The question knocked the starch out of him. As he'd been chasing after Miss Root, he'd forgotten Ma.

He'd forgotten how he'd let her down, failed to find help, and let her die. He'd let himself forget all women could be frail. So frail you could lose them at any moment and he didn't know how to save any of them. Wasn't Miss Root frailer than the rest? Hadn't he even noticed how small she'd looked in his coat, her tiny feet, the way her voice was soft. She'd even gotten chilled when it had hardly been cold. What if she got sick like Ma had and he couldn't help her, either? It could be anything.

"A little. I was eleven when Ma died." He finished unrigging the other team and hoped Barton had no more questions. The reminder of his failure sat heavy in his stomach and he no longer wanted to go in to eat.

"So you didn't see them together much? That makes it difficult, but not impossible. Look at John and Charles." Barton led the horses to their stalls.

John and Charles had both managed to find women, but Alicia and Will were nothing like Ma, especially Will, who wasn't frail in the slightest. It had been almost impossible for him to see her as a woman. He still didn't think she had any business in the barn, though Charles felt otherwise and George respected his brother.

"Why don't you let everyone know that I decided to go back to the bunkhouse." George didn't want to look at Charles and Will, and he couldn't talk to Phoebe when he was too preoccupied with his own mother.

Since Phoebe would leave in a few months, he

could go one more time to her class and read something just for her. He could let her know how he felt, but that he couldn't love a woman. Not someone frail and tender. Yet his heart only wanted her because of those very attributes. After he expressed how he felt in a way she would understand, he would stay out in the bunkhouse, avoid her completely. She would leave and he would stop thinking about her.

Eventually.

THE HOUSE HAD BEEN SO big and lonely without George, but Maretta said she shouldn't go out and look for him since she'd been feeling under the weather. All day on Friday, she'd sat in the corner of the school while Stephenia taught and waited for the hours to tick by, hoping George would come to her class.

After he'd kissed her, he'd changed. The very next day he'd shown up to help her to the wagon for church and both Eli and Arnold had been gruff with him about things that seemed inconsequential. Stephenia had been touchy with him, but had been remorseful later when George did not return to the house for the family meal.

Phoebe had sat through dinner with the family, a stranger in the middle of Olesons, and wanted to run away. Her life had not prepared her for the crush of people or rash of questions. She wanted solitude from most. Now that Stephenia had rung the bell for the end of the day, she would have a few moments of peace to rest, then people would arrive for her class. Including, hopefully, George.

Phoebe helped Stephenia arrange the stools, then sat at the teacher's desk for a moment to look over her notes. Anne came in and took off her wrap as she picked through the seats to the front of the room. She pulled up a stool and sat down, taking a deep breath.

"There may not be many attendees tonight. The doctor came back from a call this afternoon out to a house where there were complains of a severe cold. The baby turned blue and the doctor has asked that the family stay home. Some people will choose to stay away from town, others won't. We never know how fast this will spread until we're in the middle of it."

Phoebe held in the urge to cough. Just appearing sick could spread fear when it was already on the minds of so many. "If only a few people come, I'll send them home."

"Good, and if any of them seem sick, either send them with me or send them home. I'll stay as long as I can for the class, but I have a feeling I'll be spending many hours at the clinic in the coming weeks. I should see my Eli while I can."

"Do you think it will be that bad?" She knew nothing of colds or diseases. Only that they seemed to hit the poor and those with means equally hard.

"I do. I wasn't with the doctor when he went to see the baby, but a cold usually isn't bad enough that they will lose oxygen."

The door swung open again and Millie and Mrs.

Nickson appeared, along with Jasper. She'd hoped he would stay home. He had no real interest in poetry, and spending time with Millie annoyed him, making him surly.

"Good afternoon!" she called as they peeled off their layers of coats and mittens.

Anne stood and shared her news with the new arrivals, leaving Phoebe to stare at the door and wait for George. She had to see that light in his eyes once again. Had to remind herself that what she'd seen at first was there. That he did understand her. She hadn't imagined it.

The door pushed open again and Phoebe held her breath as a mother with two girls a year or two older than Millie came in and found seats. They were quiet and she didn't recognize them from weeks before. Millie approached one of the girls.

"Who are you?"

The first girl seemed completely tuckered, her eyes were only half open and though she made a valiant effort to sit nicely, she slumped in the seat. "Mable, and this is my twin Sable." Of the two, Sable was even worse. She sat with her mouth slightly open and her hair limp. Her forehead shone a layer of perspiration, even with just the lamps.

Anne approached the mother and spoke quietly. The mother cleared her throat and spoke loud enough to fill the room. "We are new in town and I signed my girls up to take the class at the clinic when I brought my baby in yesterday. They had to miss starting school this week, because they've worked so hard to get the house ready. That's the only reason we didn't come."

Anne reached out to touch the head of one of the girls and Mable's mom reached out and tugged the girl back out of reach. "They are fine."

George slipped through the door and Phoebe couldn't keep from following him with her eyes as he found a seat away from the others. Since Anne was already talking with her newest pupils, she went over to George to welcome him.

"Good afternoon. It's been a while. I'm glad you could come."

He gave her a half-smile and his glance darted to Stephenia. Phoebe promised herself that she would ask the teacher to tell him she'd been sorry for her outburst Sunday morning.

"I'm not sure how long I can stay tonight. Might only be here for the class." He arranged his belt carefully and sat on one of the stools.

"We may have to release all of you early anyway," Phoebe told him. "Anne says there's a risk of illness."

"Then you shouldn't be here." His eyes were suddenly hard and he clenched his jaw. "Women get sick too easy." He stood quickly and his eyes scanned the room, instantly falling on the two rosy-cheeked twins. "Why do you have them here? Are you trying to make the whole town sick? Get them home."

Anne stood, turning pale at his words. "George. Calm down. I'm trying to talk to them."

Instead he clenched his fists and widened his stance. "They've got no business being here if they are so sick they can barely stand. Get them out of here before everyone catches it." His chest rose and fell with heavy breaths and Phoebe reached for his arm.

"George, they're just children."

He wrenched free of her. "If you get sick, I can't help you. I don't know how." He strode over to the woman and, with jerky motions, got her and her daughters moving out of the school.

Phoebe glanced around the room at the people who were left. "I think it would be best if we just called this an evening. We'll start where we left off next week."

A shiver like ice slid up her spine and her throat burned. It would be best for her students if she listened to George's advice too, even if it meant she didn't get to see him again that night.

CHAPTER 11

After a long ride back to the Oleson ranch, Stephenia left Phoebe by the front door and drove off to find her husband. The day had gone far too long, even though she'd cut it short, and she wanted a glass of warm milk, a thick flannel wrapper, and a book to curl up with near the fire. Though all those things would be difficult to enjoy when her mind kept flitting back to George.

He'd been so angry, so pushy, just like everyone said he was before she'd come. He'd gotten the job done, getting the sick girls to go home, but his methods left much to be desired. Anne had followed George and wouldn't be home until later. George should be along shortly, but there was no reason to wait for him outside and the chill would force her indoors, where she wouldn't see him when he returned. She stood for a moment on the porch, trying to decide if she could wait a little longer in the hopes of seeing him.

Phoebe pushed the front door open and it seemed to weigh twice what she remembered. Her whole body felt both hot and cold, all at once. Will sat on a sofa in the front sitting room darning socks and rushed to help her. She slid off Phoebe's coat first, then her mittens and hat.

"You look like you've caught your death. Should've stayed home today." Will bustled her back to the kitchen and plopped her down on a stool in front of the fire. "I'll get you some warm broth going." A moment later, Will draped a thick wool blanket over her shoulders.

"You shouldn't be near me, Will. Anne says this cold could be bad, if I have what that baby in town did. I held a sick little baby last week." She closed her eyes, and her head felt tight with pressure.

"If I'm meant to get it, I will. I live in the same house as you. I'm strong, not a worry about me." Will slid a small pot on the stove and poured a jar of stock into it.

Phoebe hadn't made the time to talk to Will as Stephenia had told her to, mostly because she didn't want to listen to anything that might cloud her growing regard of George, but his actions at the school needed answers. He might be pretending, just like Robert. He might break her heart, just like Robert.

"Will, tell me about George." She let the blanket

hang on her shoulders and warmed her hands close to the stove to keep from shivering.

"That's not a story you need to hear. Just gossip anyway. Just like I told you, it's no better here than in the bunkhouse." Will stiffened slightly next to her.

"I don't mean gossip. Tonight, when he heard there might be an illness going around, he harangued a family into leaving the school because the girls had colds." Phoebe's nose burned and she sneezed.

Will handed her a kerchief from her skirt pocket and continued to warm the broth. "In fairness to George, he hasn't said anything to me of note since I lived in the bunkhouse and he has every right to have a burr under his blanket about that. I see that now. I was only looking to make my way."

So, he had treated Will as he'd treated that family. "He was rude to you then. You don't need to say more." Phoebe wiped her nose, but it didn't seem to help. The little sneeze had opened the floodgates and the longer Phoebe sat in front of the stove, the more tired she became.

"But I do. See, George is different. He isn't mean just to be mean. Every time he said something to me was because, to his mind, I was being treated differently, or trying to get away with something. In both cases, he was right. He just has a poor way of saying what he means to say. I think, in a lot of ways, he's like Charles. He hates injustice."

Like the injustice of sickness. His words rattled through her mind once more. *I can't save you…* "Perhaps he's afraid. I hate to admit that, because it doesn't seem like he would be afraid of anything, but perhaps something scares him and he gets angry instead of facing it."

"Could be. I know I'm going to have to face him at some point, because unless he leaves like John did, we'll be family. Stuck closer than honey. I can't be toeing around like I'm on eggs around him."

Phoebe let a silence fall between them because nothing more could be said. She couldn't apologize for Will's words any more than she could apologize to Will for Stephenia's. Whatever the reason, he took issue with Will and people who were ill.

"If it was that baby I held last week, then the whole school is in danger of getting it. The baby's older siblings are in Stephenia's class." Which meant Stephenia was in danger of catching it as well. "Can you please let Stephenia know I've come down with something and she should be careful?"

Phoebe no longer felt hungry enough to drink the broth. She needed to lay down under as many quilts as she could find. Her body trembled with shivers and when she stood, she pitched forward with dizziness. Will grasped her arm and dragged her back from the stove. "You get upstairs to your bed. I'll bring this up and a hot pan for under your quilt. I'll let Stephenia know and maybe find Anne. They may have to close the school next week if it might spread through the children."

Phoebe slowly made her way up the stairs, her head pitching as she walked. George would think it was his fault she was sick, he'd blame himself for taking her for the ride and for not getting the children out of the school fast enough. She closed her eyes and rested for a moment on the stairs. When she got better, she would need to talk with him. Sickness happened and there wasn't always anything that could be done.

She found her bed and pulled back the blankets. After struggling with her boots for a moment, she got them off and curled up in her bed with the wool blanket she'd gotten in the kitchen still wrapped around her. If only she could rest and get better, then she could let George see there was nothing to fear.

CHAPTER 12

The bunkhouse had always seemed like a fine place to be. It served its purpose as the place George hung his hat, talked to the other hands, and saw his brother. But as he strode in after getting those sick children to leave the school, the bunkhouse wasn't what he needed and he knew it.

Charles sat at the scarred wooden table and tossed a hand of Patience down. "Evening, I didn't expect you back so soon."

"The reading was canceled. There are some sick children in town. Phoebe didn't look well." He peeled off his ranch coat and hung it up beside his hat. "What if she gets sick? Or all the women out here? Well, except Will, she won't. Not like she's frail." He tossed his hands in the air.

"Just what are you saying, George? You think illness would just skip over Will, or do you have a reason for thinking she's not just as weak to illness as anyone else?" Charles stood and faced him.

He wasn't looking for a fight, he only wanted to make sure Phoebe didn't get anything. She was too tiny, too frail, too…womanly. "She's just strong, more man than woman."

Charles narrowed his eyes and flexed his jaw, choosing his words carefully. "Just because you didn't notice she was a woman right away, doesn't make her any less a woman. Maybe you didn't care to notice, but our father was a man and he was strong and hale until the lung sickness."

It wasn't that he hadn't cared about his own father, but he'd barely known his pa by the time he died. Natalie was the one who spoke to him and tried to get him to take account of George and his brothers, but Pa hadn't done it. He'd ignored them.

"George, are you saying Pa was womanly?" Charles shook him by the shoulders, pulling him out of his thoughts.

"I didn't say any such thing." Though he did realize now that his ideas where illness, his father, and Will were concerned were muddled. "I don't know how to feel about Will, and I don't know what to say about Pa. I just know it scares me to death to think about Phoebe getting sick."

"None of us want to see anyone get sick. We were all old enough to remember Ma."

But no one knew how he'd tried to help. No one knew he'd failed. He should've gone for a doctor instead of allowing Pa to worry about the cost. He could've agreed to work to bring a doctor in. Pa wouldn't do it, but *he* could've. Instead, he'd tried to think of a way to do it without money, as if Ma hadn't been worth every bit.

"I can't make you like Will. I can't make you treat her better. But when you talked to Barton about wanting respect, you missed the mark. I can't respect you if you treat my future wife like she isn't worth the dirt on your boot, simply because she pulled the wool over your eyes. She's a good woman, and a good rancher. You'll see that if you ever give her a chance.

"You want us to respect you, start treating all of us with respect. You've been trying so hard to do what's right around that teacher, but forgetting about how you treated everyone else in your past. There's a reason Stephenia jumped on you like a wolf before church on Sunday. You've earned it. Will avoids you after what you said to her when she worked as a hand. You need to make those things right first."

"Everything I think about women is framed around the two I grew up with, Ma and Natalie. Ma was frail, small. I remember her being not so much taller than me right before she died. Natalie was no woman, she was a bossy sister."

Charles sat back down in front of his game, but did not move to play. "So, you see most women as small and almost sickly, because that's how you remember Ma. Except for those with a backbone, those you see like Natalie?"

He hadn't put it in so many words before, but he could see it now as truth. Will bothered him because she was like Natalie. His sister could whittle, form wood into prosthetics, drive a team of horses, hitch anything that moved, all because she'd had to. She wouldn't get sick either, by his estimation. "I suppose I do see it that way, yes."

"There are many types of women in this world. Just like there are many ways to reach the same destination. If it changes how you feel about Natalie, she understood why you treated her so poorly. She only tried to be Ma so we didn't feel the loss like she did. She thought she was helping."

"She will never know." And neither would Charles, because the secret was his alone. She'd only made it worse, pretending to be a mother he didn't deserve. Salting his wounds every time she got bossy.

"Maybe not, but doesn't it help to see it from her side? And can you see how Will needed to act as she did? So she could earn the money for her own ranch? She had to act as a man. No one was going to let her be a roper if she didn't."

Though it pained him to admit he'd been wrong, he could. "I'm sorry."

"Tell Will, not me."

He slapped his hat on his head, ready to turn the world around. Taking on the mother at the school had felt like he'd done something positive for Phoebe, something in the right direction. He was antsy right down to his boots to do more. "I'll do just that."

George made it halfway to the house before his feet slowed. He'd never really taken it upon himself to apologize for his behavior because, to his own mind, it had seemed right, justified. Certainly true. Will had bothered him from the moment they met because she seemed to be taking advantage of his cousin and his uncle. Now, he could see that Will hadn't been taking advantage, but it had taken looking at it through his brother's eyes to see that. He couldn't do that with every problem. He had to have his own intuition. What if all his ideas were wrong? Where would that land him?

He pushed on ahead and instead of knocking, just went inside. Nathen stood by the fireplace in the sitting room, smoking a pipe. He usually only had one on Sunday evenings and it stopped George short. There had to be something wrong.

"George, good to see you. What brings you in?"

He swallowed hard and raked the hat off his head. He was still getting used to manners in the house, not that Aunt Maretta would let him forget. "I came to talk to Will, if she's still awake. I know it's later in the evening."

Nathen nodded and his expression went sober. "She's upstairs with Miss Root. Seems she's come down with a powerful cold. Will asked Maretta to stay away."

So, he'd been right. She was sick. "May I go up and see her and talk to Will? It's important." Perhaps not gravely, but if he didn't talk now, he might change his mind. Tonight he not only had the desire to do what was right, but the opportunity, and that couldn't be wasted.

"The door is open. Keep still though. Miss Root

needs her rest. If she can't teach, she'll have no money. She told me her benefactor still hasn't sent her pay and I know Dr. Spight sent the money to have her come to Belle Fourche."

Without money, she couldn't leave either. "I won't be long. Thank you, sir."

"George?" Nathen asked, before he could leave. "I had planned to send you off to see a friend of mine in the spring. I was worried you just weren't fitting in here, no matter the rules we set or the example. But over the last few weeks, I've gotten a hint of improvement. Less anger. Keep it up son. Your father would be proud."

The words stopped him cold. He'd never thought he'd ever hear that his father was proud, had given up ever hearing it after he died. Once he did hear it though, he realized that was exactly what he'd been so angry about. His father had never taken notice of anything he'd done. He'd never noticed George had run off to save Ma by getting medicine, he'd never noticed the wood box full of firewood, or the way he fed the horses. So, he'd gotten bitter and quit doing the jobs.

"Thank you, sir." Part of the anger he'd been coddling let loose and George took a breath of free air for a moment as he made his way up the stairs.

A door stood open at the end of the second-floor hall on the women's side of the house. He slowly strode down, trying to keep his boots and spurs from clicking on the wood floor. The talking in the room stopped as he approached.

Will sat by Phoebe's bed. As usual, she wore a plain white shirtwaist with a plain skirt, never wanting to draw attention to herself. Her hair was in braids and curled around her head in a circle like an angel's halo. She turned and her lips flattened. As he took a moment to really look at her—because he'd avoided the practice since finding out who she was—he could see Charles was right. She was every bit a woman, with fine cheekbones and soft green eyes.

"Miss Will, may I speak to you for a moment?" He didn't feel he knew her well enough anymore to just call her William as he had in the bunkhouse. She seemed a completely different person now and he needed to act like she was.

She stood and came the few steps out to meet him. "Is something wrong with Charles?" Her eyes raked his face and her brow furrowed.

"No, Charles is fine. I didn't mean to worry you. I…" He was immediately distracted by the bundle of blankets on the bed, covering Phoebe. "Is she…?"

"Feverish, talking nonsense," Will filled in. "What do you need?" Her words were short, clipped, and she didn't look him directly in the eye. He couldn't blame her.

"Miss Will." Barton's words came back to him about buttering Lula's hair. Barton had done what was right, and so could he. "I done you wrong when you worked as a hand, and especially after. I hope you can find it in your heart to forgive me. I'm doing my best to become someone my uncle can be proud of, and how I acted wasn't that way." He held his breath for a second. He'd figured she'd try to box his ears or something and maybe he deserved it, but over the last three weeks, he'd been pure educated on the way of the world. He'd learned that what men said over a game of cards didn't make them respectable. It was what they did to make life better for others. He'd learned he didn't see women the way they should be seen, there were more than two kinds. And mostly, he'd learned even if he tried to avoid women because they were frail and weak, it still hurt when he thought about losing them. Especially one in particular.

He'd fallen in love with Phoebe without even trying.

"I understand, George. Most of what happened was just talk."

"Poor talk isn't right and what I said was out of confusion and misunderstanding."

Will nodded. "I should get back in with her. That fever can't be left untended."

He froze and gripped her arm. "What can I do?"

"Tomorrow, at first light, you might want to get the doctor. I think we're going to need him."

CHAPTER 13

George took Will's suggestion to get the doctor seriously. Phoebe hadn't even pushed back the blanket the night before to see him. Her sickness was too much like Ma's. This time he would do what was right and get the doctor. This time he would make them come and see her.

He strode into the barn to get his horse and found Stephenia sitting on a stool near an empty horse stall. She cradled her head in her hands. He didn't want to disturb her, nor did he need to hear any more from her about how he should act. She'd scolded him enough for two sisters.

He strode past her and went to fetch Jerky's saddle.

"George? Might I have a word with you?"

He flinched at Stephenia's voice. How he'd hoped she would just ignore him.

"Yes, ma'am. Though I am in a bit of a hurry. I need to get the doctor for Phoebe. Will asked me to."

He needed to add that so Stephenia didn't assume he'd decided to go all on his own.

But instead of chastising him, she nodded with understanding. "She looked like she might be taking ill last night when I brought her home. Anne asked me not to go to school this morning and said she'd put a note on the door of the school. Late last night, that little baby died." Stephenia pressed her hand to her belly and then reached out and caught his arm. "Life is too short and too precious for me to hold a grudge, George. You never did anything to me, but I saw the trouble you were giving my husband and I wanted to punish some sense into you. Since you weren't one of my students, I didn't know how to do it.

"I was rude to you. When I caught you kissing Phoebe. At first, I wanted to break you two apart and haul you back to the barn. But I've talked to Arnold since then and he tells me he's seen great progress in you, and that it might be thanks to Phoebe. I'm sorry, George. The idea that I could've destroyed with my words what you've worked so hard for, tears me up. Please, forgive me."

He didn't have time to explain to her he was still working on getting better, and he certainly didn't want to tell her that, despite his kiss, Phoebe wouldn't stay in Belle Fourche. She'd only talked about leaving and poetry, not feelings. Especially for him. She'd seen a gift that didn't exist, and once he'd disavowed her of that notion, she'd had little time for him.

"I wish I could claim there was something to destroy, but I can't. I stole that kiss and I shouldn't have done it. Now I'm trying to make it right by getting the doctor. I'm probably no better now than what you thought of me before." He certainly didn't feel any better. No matter how hard he worked, Phoebe would still be weak. Even if she survived her sickness, she would still leave once spring came around.

He saddled Jerky and rushed as fast as he dared on the long ride. Once he reached town, it was quiet. No one walked down the streets. There were no horses waiting for riders outside the line of businesses on Main Street. He rode slowly through town, looking for signs that anyone was there. Many of the businesses had hung signs in the windows saying they were closed temporarily. Word of illness had spread fast. Thank the Lord everyone had taken it seriously.

He tied Jerky in front of the little clinic and rushed for the door. Inside, he found rows of cots, full of cowboys he recognized from one ranch on the north side of town. In the corner lay the two girls he'd rooted out of the school. Dr. Spight knelt beside one of the cots and Anne stood amid the cots with a metal bucket of water and a dipper. She finished bringing water to that row then came over to him.

"Stay back, at least ten feet from any of the cots and ten feet from me as well."

He couldn't stay away, he had to bring Anne or the doctor back to the ranch. "I can't. Phoebe needs you."

Anne shook her head and her gray eyes seemed deep, tired. "I can't, George. I shouldn't even allow you to leave now that you've come through the door.

We've got room upstairs if you're willing to stay with her and do as I tell you to. But neither the doctor, nor I, can leave the clinic until all the fevers break." She wiped her forehead with the back of her arm.

He glanced all over the room and noticed a line of women along the back. "No…too many families will be hit. What if she doesn't make it, what if I can't help her, just like my Ma?"

Anne led him over to the huge front window and sat him down at the bench there. "You tried to help save your ma?"

He stared over at all the people laying in the beds and he stood right back up. "You don't have time for me right now. These people need you."

"Do you think the people in this room got here because no one cared for them?"

He knew the mother of the girls in the corner cared, but it hadn't stopped them from getting sick. The poor baby who had died was cared for. "I didn't say that. I tried to help my ma, but what I got for her didn't work. I couldn't get her a doctor, and now the only way I can get one for Phoebe is by bringing her where everyone is sick. What if my choice kills her? What if it's my fault that I lose someone else?" He gnawed on his lip. Men didn't cry, and he wouldn't. No matter how badly he hurt at the thought of losing Phoebe before she understood what she'd done for him. How much she'd helped him.

Anne shot to her feet and shook him by the arms. "Look around you! Take a good look. Most of these people did nothing wrong. They ate with someone who didn't seem sick, they helped someone who was. They went about their day. People fall ill, and some die. No matter if I'm standing beside their bed or not. Sickness doesn't pick and choose. It's a horrible thing but it's part of this fallen world we live in. You can live your life utterly alone to avoid it, or trust that no one dies without fulfilling their purpose.

"You did not kill your mother, George. It can seem terribly unfair, when sickness creeps up on the unsuspecting, leaving behind those who could never be prepared for a loss. It tears you to pieces. I look around this room and don't even try to guess who might be the most ill. I merely treat all that I can, give all that I can, and pray for each and every one of them."

He'd done just that with his mother. "And do you ever wish you'd done more?"

Anne closed her eyes and let out a harsh breath. "Of course. Who wouldn't? But I cannot change the Lord's timing any more than you can. I can neither steal, nor add, a moment to their time here. I take heart in that. It's all I can do. It's all *you* can do."

He hadn't wanted to risk bringing Phoebe in, but she couldn't get help unless he did. He would have to stay with her, now that he'd been near Anne. "My choice is to bring her."

"Aye, you will. And you won't leave once you do. You've been in here, too close to me, so now you must remain quarantined with us. Don't go near Maretta or anyone else at the ranch. Warn them just like I did with you. You bundle up Phoebe and bring her here.

Have one of your brothers come to get your horse. As far as we know, it can't be spread through animals."

He clenched his jaw and nodded. He hadn't planned to leave her side anyway. He hated pushing his horse to ride again so soon after such a race into town, but he'd expected to leave his horse there and ride back out with the doctor. Now, he'd have to hitch a wagon when he got back and make sure Phoebe got to town, all without coming within ten feet of anyone.

Though he couldn't race Jerky or risk losing him. He made it back to the ranch before lunch. Charles strode into the barn as he dismounted. "Stay back. I've been to town to see the doctor. Can you take care of Jerky and hitch me a rig to bring Phoebe into town?"

Charles nodded simply and waited by the door. Once George dismounted, he left, giving his brother a wide gap. "Tell Conrad that I'll be in town, under quarantine. Whoever goes in to get the horse and wagon will need to stay outside the clinic. Don't go in."

Charles nodded as he took up the reins. "Understood. Be careful."

He wasn't worried about himself. Only Phoebe, those children already sick, and the row of women in the back of the clinic. Who would help them? He headed for the house. Getting inside without going near anyone in there would be the biggest problem. While the rooms were large enough, there were hallways where people could catch you unawares. He'd have to be extra careful.

As he pushed open the door, Will headed for him. He held up a hand to stop her and she nodded her understanding. "She's still up in her room, but hasn't eaten since last night. She's still talking nonsense about teaching, and not teaching."

He gulped back his trepidation. If Phoebe had mentioned him, Will would say it.

"She compares you to someone named Robert," Will went on. "From what I've gathered, he was false with her. Lied to her to get her attention."

Acid built in his stomach. His rash need to steal a kiss could have made her think he was just like whoever Robert was. Phoebe could already believe he didn't care about her except for a kiss. Just like Barton had warned him. "What she talks about when her brain is addled with fever isn't my concern. I just need to get her to the doctor so she has the chance to tell me what she thinks in her right mind."

Will nodded and pursed her lips. "I've been with her all night. I shouldn't stay here where I can get Charles, Nathen, and Maretta sick. Take me with you. I can help Anne if I don't catch ill."

Her logic was sound. "Charles is out hitching the wagon. Say your goodbyes for now, but don't go near him. I'll be out shortly with Phoebe."

Will let him go up the stairs and he heard the door slam shut as she left. The upstairs was silent and it made his skin crawl with worry. If Maretta had already been infected by checking on Phoebe, the whole ranch would get sick. She was the glue that bound everyone together. Could she have stayed away from her guest when Phoebe was so sick?

He slowly stepped into Phoebe's room and she stared at him, her eyes glassy and face flushed. "I didn't think you wanted to see me anymore." A hoarse whisper rasped from her lips.

"I'm sorry I let you think that, but I've got to get you into the doctor now. You and I, we're going to take a ride in the wagon. Maybe Miss Will can drive and I'll sit in the back with you and keep you all bundled up tight."

"It's too cold to go out." She closed her eyes and he strode the rest of the way to the bed.

Her soft speech and flushed face worried him. She had to get to the doctor, so he could do everything possible to help her.

"It's not as chilly as yesterday. You've got to go in and see Anne. She's expecting you." And him. He tucked the quilts around her legs and lifted her, ignoring her squeal of protest.

"The bed is warm. I know I'll get better. George, please." Though her words fought against him, she did not.

"I'm sorry, Phoebe. This time, I fight for the woman I love."

CHAPTER 14

Phoebe lay in her bed as George sat next to her. Sometimes he spoke, other times he just held her hand. She'd been angry with him at first for bringing her to Dr. Spight when others needed the doctor more, but the doctor had told her she was wrong almost from the start. He'd started her on something to help break the fever. It was a new medicine, and very bitter. But more bitter even than the medicine, was the realization that though George loved her, he still wanted her to go.

He'd told her about his mother, how he'd failed her and let her die. He'd also told her that in helping her, he was making right what he'd done. He'd spent the last three weeks trying to make his life right, to impress her. Which made her see that what she'd seen was false, in a sense. Though he was trying. He hadn't been hiding who he was, just trying to do better. It was commendable. Except that was where it ended.

Women died. If they didn't get sick and die, they could die in childbirth, or fire, or accidentally and he couldn't open his heart to that again. He'd told her so. He'd held her hand against his heart and felt the trembling as he'd said she had to move on. She'd worked hard to get better, but his talk made her want to roll over and give up.

"If you're going to leave me as soon as I'm better, you might as well just go. The longer you sit here, the more I care about you. If I'm going to die, just let me die alone. You give me no hope to look forward to. You act as if I should get well just so you can put me on a train. There's more to life than survival. Life is love. Love is sacrifice. If you can't see that, then you didn't love me to begin with." She tugged her hand from his and tried to roll over, but the blankets were too tight around her and she still wasn't strong enough to fight against their weight.

"I lost my mother when I was eleven years old, Phoebe. Then had to live with the guilt every time I saw my father. Before Ma died, he was happy. We were a family. He cared. When Ma died, nothing mattered but the one who was missing."

"He grieved and forced you to become a man when you weren't ready." Phoebe tucked her hand under the blanket to keep him from reaching for it again. His touch was so tender it broke her heart. She ached to have him near always, and he wouldn't be.

"I think he wished he could've died right alongside her. I think he saw us as a curse, at least, us boys.

Natalie was old enough to take care of herself. I hated her for still having a bond with Pa."

"Hate will get you nowhere. I know. I hated Robert, too. I hated him for lying to me, and for taking my family from me. He's probably working for my father now. No matter that he tricked me."

"I didn't trick you. Never."

She closed her eyes and prayed that was true. "What about when you first came to see me read? When I stopped you from leaving?"

He chuckled and she loved the sound. "That wasn't the first time I saw you. I followed you that very day you arrived and I snuck into your reading the week before you saw me, just so I could listen."

"I didn't see you that day. The room was so full." She tried to recall, but her head hurt as she tried to think.

"I wanted to listen to you, to hear your voice. When you read, it makes my heart pump faster and I feel it. I guess you thought I had a gift because I wanted to be there so badly, but I don't. I just wanted to see you and hear you read, to be close to you. No different than any of those other cowboys." He leaned back in his seat and crossed his arms. Though he hadn't left when she'd told him to, she could feel a distance between them.

"I saw that feeling in your eyes, and I knew you had a gift because of your words. You can deny them if you wish, but I'm too tired to argue with you about what I know is there." She tried again, unsuccessfully, to roll away from him. So he could leave without having to look her in the eye to do it.

"The sisters were sent home this morning. Everyone downstairs is slowly getting better." He was tired, she could hear it in the depth of his voice. "They let Will go home this morning. I was right, she never did get sick."

"But all those cowboys down there did, so don't tell me this illness only chose the weak."

He leaned forward, letting his head rest in his palm. "I know what you're trying to do. The doctor says since you never got your pay, he's going to pay your way to the Normal School."

"So that's it? You're just going to kiss me and send me off? You're going to be just like every other man? Nothing special." Her heart ached at the injustice and she wanted to cry, but that would only force him into guilt. That wasn't what she was after. She wanted his heart, for him to beg her to stay. She'd been in love with Robert at first, or thought she was. He'd swept her away. "You were my first kiss, George. I hadn't planned to until I married. Now, I may never again."

He slid his hand through his hair and glanced away from her. "I don't know what to do. I want to hold you close, keep you, protect you, make you mine. But there's so much that's out of my control."

"Life never was fully in your control." When she hadn't received her payment and had been faced with very few choices, that had become clear.

He stroked her cheek and smiled. "It finally broke. Your fever is gone."

She closed her eyes. "I guess this is goodbye then."

He nodded and stood. "As soon as Dr. Spight says you're fine to go back to the ranch, I'll come and get you."

Everything inside her crashed into a black hole. She couldn't live on the ranch and see him every day, especially when she only worked on Fridays. She would have to hide not to see him. "I'll just have the doctor put me back up in the boarding house."

"Are you…cert—" He didn't finish. Instead, he turned and left her laying there as a tear rolled down her cheek and a sob broke free from her chest since she no longer had to hold it in.

School started back up the day after George had left Phoebe's side. Stephenia had brought all of Phoebe's belongings down to her wagon to take to her at the boarding house. He'd watched her drive off with Phoebe's trunk and an emptiness filled his chest he hadn't ever felt before. Phoebe wasn't coming back. Even losing his mother hadn't felt the same. That had been final, Phoebe's loss was tinged with a bitter hope that she might ignore him and someday return.

He kicked a rock loose and it went flying down the drive. He felt just like that. Like someone had decided he didn't belong where he'd been put and kicked him out. But did he have the power to change it? Phoebe had said he didn't have control over much of anything, and she was right to a point. He couldn't control where his life might end up. But he had learned that he could control how he acted and whether or not it was worthy of respect. He could control whether he chose to be afraid or not. Being afraid didn't feel half so bad as the gut twisting loss of Phoebe.

That one woman had done more to change him than all the rules, all the arm-pulling, and all the work Conrad and his cousins had given him. She'd given him a reason to change. He wanted to be a better man so she would notice him, and so others would think he was worthy of her, but was he? Had he done enough, was it ever enough?

The Good Book said a man wasn't saved by works and that was true in the eyes of the Lord, but the eyes of men were different. Men didn't forget a slight.

Even that didn't hold up to his old measuring stick though, because Stephenia had forgiven him. She'd gone out of her way to be kind to him when Phoebe hadn't returned to the ranch with him. Everyone seemed to understand that he'd gone there not because he was ill, but to be with her while she was, and he'd come home empty-handed.

The old George would've taken out his anger on some unsuspecting person who happened to get in his way. Now, he just wanted to be alone and think. Phoebe wasn't going to leave Belle Fourche for a few months, but that didn't mean he should take all that time to decide. She could turn away from him completely and refuse to see him.

Anne drove up the drive, still looking worn from

her work at the clinic. She waved to him, then pulled the wagon to a stop in front of him. "George, good to see you."

He'd gotten to know her better at the clinic, since he, the doctor, Anne, and Will were the only ones well enough to talk. He nodded in response.

"I wanted to thank you for your help with Phoebe, and even hauling water when we needed. It was such a help to Dr. Spight and I. I wish we'd managed to save Edgar. His memorial will be tomorrow."

George had been so focused on Phoebe, he hadn't even been aware they'd lost anyone except the baby. "I'm sorry."

She took a deep breath and gathered the lines. "I stopped by to see Phoebe. She's doing well, in case you were wondering." She flicked the leather lines and the horses continued on to the barn.

The only loss at the clinic had been Edgar, a cowboy. A young man with many years ahead of him. He would never find love, never own land, never do the things he enjoyed. He'd been healthy, not weak.

How could he think for a moment that life would be better for him without Phoebe? He was already hurting like she'd left him for good and she hadn't even left Belle Fourche. How could his first thought of the lost cowboy be "he would never find love", if it wasn't more important than loss?

He couldn't lose Phoebe by choice. That was even worse than losing her by chance.

CHAPTER 15

Phoebe paced her usual spot in front of the school. They had only missed one week of poetry, the week George had shown, in the only way he knew how, that he would protect her no matter the cost to his own reputation. She stared at her pocket watch as the minutes ticked by. The hour for the start of class passed and she tapped her fingers against the desk. No students came to her class.

"I guess people are too busy getting caught up with the work they missed. So many families were ill or had workers who were ill for almost a week." Stephenia added a log to the fire to chase away the growing chill.

Phoebe tightened her shawl and pinned it closed. "I suppose you're right. I'd just hoped to have at least one student." The one she'd been thinking about since the last she'd seen him just a few days before. The one who wouldn't come, because he'd already said goodbye.

"Dare I hope you mean George?" Stephenia sat down on a stool facing her and smiled. "I've spoken to him almost every single day. He's changed quite drastically. Though, he's very quiet of late."

She nodded, but didn't give in to her desire to ask more. He'd made it plain that he wanted her to leave, so she had. If he'd wanted to see her, he knew where she was.

"And if he did come tonight, what would you do?" Stephenia pressed.

"I would…" Fall into his embrace and cry? That's what she'd wanted to do all week. Her heart was just empty. Even poetry didn't help. It was nothing but words now. "Walk away." Though, she didn't want to. It was what he wanted her to do, because he'd said it was better for both of them. Though her heart didn't believe it for a moment. If his did, she couldn't fight it.

"Do you mean that?" Stephenia asked.

"Why are you asking me? You didn't even think he was a respectable man until he brought me in to the clinic." It still chafed that Stephenia stopped the one kiss she would ever have, and before *she* was done. Since no one had attended her class, she would have to consider leaving early. Her stomach clenched tightly, and she blinked to keep her tears at bay.

"I'm asking because I see you both moping about like there's nothing to be done when there's most certainly something. You can talk to him."

No, she'd tried that. She'd reasoned with him in

A LADY LOVES MUCH

the clinic as soon as her mind had been clear enough to think. He'd still left. There was no reasoning with him.

"He's far too stubborn for that."

Stephenia went around her desk and pulled out a drawer with a few books in it. "If you won't listen to reason, then I'll use this time to read. You are welcome to half my ham from lunch. I didn't have the stomach for the whole thing."

The minutes ticked by and Phoebe nibbled on the ham while trying to focus on her reading. Without any students, she would have to provide something for the reading. Everyone would be watching her for as long as she could stand to be there. And they would be disappointed, because her heart was gone.

People slowly poured into the little school and filled the seats for the reading. Not one single Oleson came and she took a deep breath. It hadn't snowed yet. She could make it to the Normal School if they were ready for her early, or maybe she could wire her benefactor and head back to Alabama or even South Carolina during the winter months. Anywhere but Belle Fourche and the Olesons.

The door closed again and she turned to take her seat. George stood by the door in his Sunday best suit and her knees lost all fortitude. She gripped the stool tightly and couldn't speak, her mouth went dry.

"Miss Root." He nodded, tugging his hat off his head. He'd gotten a haircut and had gotten his two bits worth. His lips had been covered before by his unwillingness to shave daily, but now they were perfect, clean-shaven, and turned upward in a slight smile directed at her.

"Mr. Oleson," she let out on a breath.

"I thought I'd come read for you, if you don't mind." He strode forward as if she'd already given her permission and she felt every ounce of the desire to do what was right, to tell him to leave, then flee herself.

"Certainly." She handed him her book and he took it, then set it on the desk.

He leaned against it casually and crossed his arms, far too close to her. His scent caressed her senses and she closed her eyes for a moment.

"I call this one, *New*." He cleared his throat and stared straight into her eyes as if they were the only ones in the room, without thirty other people gaping at them.

"Without you, my old life overpowers me.

Without you, I cannot face the day.

I look to my honor to do what is right, and it fails me.

I look to my fellow man to guide me and they have no advice."

He grasped her hand and slid down onto one knee. "I can't live in the old for a moment longer. Don't make me keep seeking for what my heart knows I've already found. I told you once that if you loved something, you wouldn't let it wear you thin. You would learn to love it more. Have I worn you too thin? Or can you learn to love me for the rest of our lives, Phoebe Root?"

The room erupted in gasps, and Phoebe glanced

around them, heat burning up her neck. He'd come back, and he'd said he loved her, wanted her forever, within a poem. He *did* understand her poet's heart.

"I think I've learned to love you much more than I ever dreamed, George."

He smiled from his spot on the floor. "So, what say you?"

The word "yes" sounded so dull in light of how he'd proposed, but she could think of no other. "Yes."

Everyone in the room cheered as George shot to his feet and wrapped her in his arms. She'd waited all week to feel him, sense him, smell him, even taste him. She laid her hands on his cheeks, which were soft as they'd ever been, and pulled his face to hers.

This time, she wasn't about to let Stephenia stop her.

EPILOGUE

The stifling July heat bore down on the train as it headed for the station in Belle Fourche. Her heart raced in time with the *chug* of the wheels. Only a few more minutes.

She and George had spent all winter, one of the times with the least amount of work on a ranch, courting. Once the spring had come, they had decided she would still go to the Normal School, since she'd already signed on for the job and it was a matter of her word. While she was gone, George was going to build a house on the little parcel of land Uncle Nathen had given him and they would be ready to marry.

Though she still loved poetry, it had become secondary to her. George was her first love and they discussed everything. He loved to listen to her read, but he admitted he knew nothing about writing poetry, nor did he really want to read it on his own. He liked it because she did, and his honesty had made her love him all the more.

The little steeple on the church appeared on the horizon and she almost bounced in her seat. The plan had been that she would return, then the following Friday, she and George would wed in a small ceremony at the church. But she'd been held in Spearfish for two days longer than she'd planned and now her wedding day would be the day after she arrived. There was much to prepare for, and no time.

Phoebe tugged her little carpet bag close to her and tried to see the reflection of her hair in the window. The red tended to look sickly if she got ash in it from the train. There was no way to really tell in the window.

As the train bore down on the station, she clutched tight to her bag and tried not to count the minutes. The train pulled in and she was the first to stand and the first to rush to the platform. The porter helped her over the deep chasm between the train and the platform. There, waiting for her, was every Oleson, including Stephenia with a brand new little bundle. Anne now had a soft mound on her own belly that she wasn't even trying to hide. Lula held the hands of her twins. One of them reached around to hug her, pulling her own rounded belly into relief.

Charles was there with Will, their arms draped casually around each other. Even John and Alicia were there with fresh new clothes and big smiles.

"Where are Cody and Natalie?" she asked as she

rushed up to the group. They were the only members of the family who seemed to be missing.

George met her and pulled the bag out of her hands, then kissed her gently, stealing away her thoughts of everyone around her. "I've missed you," he whispered.

"And I, you." She held him closer, reveling in the feel of his strength next to her, his arms around her. She never wanted to be apart from him again.

"Cody and Nat will be along in a bit. It's not comfortable for him to stand around for long periods, and we couldn't guarantee the train would be on time. They are probably already at the church."

"The church?" She touched her hair, sure it was a mess after the long ride. It was only Thursday. There shouldn't have been a service for anyone that day.

"Yes, O'Hare is waiting there for us. The house is built and I'm itching to carry you across that threshold."

She felt the heat rush up her neck. "That's why everyone is here?"

"Why come to town twice? Since we were already meeting you, today seemed a good day to do it." He squeezed her hand. "Have you changed your mind?"

She rested her head against his shoulder for just a moment as she let it sink in that she didn't have to wait even one more day. "Never. I will never have to search for a family again."

ALSO BY KARI TRUMBO

Need a Book fix? I've got a series within a series in Blessings, Calif. Keep scrolling to read the first chapter, or get your copy now!

This is the last in the Brothers of Belle Fourche series, but don't miss where the South Dakota stories all began, with the

Seven Brides of South Dakota

Dreams in Deadwood

Kisses in Keystone

[Love in Lead](#)

[Romance in Rapid](#)

[Sparks in Spearfish](#)

[Hearts in Hot Springs](#)

[Courting in Custer](#)

A review is an author's lifeline. It often helps us know what to write next. If you enjoyed this or any of my stories, please let me know. I want to keep writing what you want to read.

BLESSED BEYOND MEASURE

The Steamboat Sophie,
Winter 1850

Lenora clutched her shawl about her shoulders at the rail of the ship as the wind whipped her skirts about her ankles. Cold sea air drove spray into her face, but she no longer felt it. Her little room was too cramped to stay inside. And there was the scenery above … not just the endless ocean, but the man who'd started invading her every waking thought.

The waves rocked the steamer, but her stomach had long-since tired of trying to feel at-ease. If anything, the longer she was aboard ship, the more she detested it and would never offer to board again, not that it mattered. They were on their way to California, land of a million dreams, and there she would remain.

Blessings ... she'd clutched to the name like a life raft since they'd left so long ago.

She'd heard rumors while standing at that very spot by the rail, rumors of landfall at the Isthmus of Panama. After six months at sea, solid land beneath her feet would be a blessed treat. It didn't matter that she'd also heard of rats the size of small dogs, bugs that could kill her, and monkeys that screamed loud enough to be heard miles away. It was land, and solid ground would mean her stomach could stop pitching.

Seven months before, in the early spring, her father had received a message from an old associate in need of help in California. Mr. Winslet had requested they come *post haste* to help him in building a land office in the new town of Blessings. He had miners that came and went aplenty, but he was looking to make Blessings into more than just a mining town. Mr. Winslet had a dream of building a place where people would be happy, share life, and grow old with him. Her father had made the decision, almost overnight, that they would all go. After a month of selling everything they wouldn't need and hiring two men to come with them as protection, they'd left everything she knew behind.

In a new town, Lenora could finally escape the expectation that she would be little more than a pretty face for a future husband to dote over and pat on the head. Her father had tried to rein in her pesky desires to become a lawyer like himself, but that had only made her crave it more. She could stretch herself, do something with the talents the Lord had given her. Be something in a little town that would expect every member to pull their weight to make it a success. After so many months at sea, she would never offer to return; Boston never held her heart, but the little town she'd never seen, did.

Mr. Abernathy was late. She'd have to go back below soon, or her mother would turn furious. A quick glance behind her, and she turned back to the vast ocean to hide her smile. Victor Abernathy approached with his usual swagger. Her skin prickled to life, just as it would if the sun had landed upon her. Anticipation of verbally sparring with him heated her up more than her thin shawl ever could. He was a man well used to anyone's bed but his own, or so he claimed, and he'd been pestering her almost from the start. Whenever her father wasn't around to take notice, he would appear.

Though she'd always been told she was beautiful, she'd never attracted the attention of a man with such an air of danger about him. His dark caramel hair had grown long on the ship, but he didn't seem to mind, using it instead to appear even more devilishly handsome as it whipped around his face in the blustery gale. He leaned against the rail next to her, confidence the very fiber of his clothing. His eyes, greener than the sea, ablaze just for her, took her in with an appreciative nod. No, this man wasn't for her. But keeping him away was a wonderful daily challenge that drove her to seek the open space of the deck whenever the weather would permit, and even like today, when it was questionable.

"Miss Farnsworth, pleasant day." He tipped his bowler hat and let his jade eyes wander liberally over her face, almost like a true caress.

"Some might claim it. It seemed rather cool to me." The rumor of land had said that it would get warmer as they approached landfall, but without that hope, the sea still left her cold to the bone.

She pulled the shawl tighter. There was nothing decent about Victor Abernathy, and if she knew what was good for her, she'd stay away. So, why did she always find herself at the rail, looking over her shoulder to see if he would draw near, hoping he would notice her standing there? He was so very different from all the men her father had introduced her to, hoping to build business relations between families. Abernathy was exciting, and completely forbidden. He stood too close to her, spoke flippantly, and didn't hide his tendencies nor his desires, like so many other men did.

Her father had hired him and another man, Cort, to accompany them to California. The other man stayed mostly hidden, watching them from a distance. She forgot about him most of the time. But not Abernathy. He was far from subtle. Every day, just when she was sure he wasn't going to come pester her that day, he would appear. And before they finished speaking, he'd have her heart beating erratically with his witty banter. No man from Boston had ever done that.

"Come now, my lovely, is my company so poor that you can't even have a smile when I'm about?

Even a little one? Have a care, and tip those lovely lips just for me."

He moved to lean his hip against the railing and she fought the urge to push him off into the churning waters. Then his pestering would stop. But she wouldn't, because, despite what she made him think, no one had ever challenged her like Mr. Abernathy. Nor could anyone make her feel alive as he did. There was little doubt that he'd also *offered his time* to other women on the ship, which had made his pursuit of her less special, but he *was* a cad. Either she could allow herself to enjoy the mental stimulation of his visits, or let her mind wander to how many skirts he'd chased and let it get to her. She'd chosen to ignore his ignoble pastimes and enjoy the stolen moments he spent with her, chaste though they were.

"My father hired you to watch over my family. My *entire* family, Mr. Abernathy. I would think you would be a little more serious."

He sighed, and his firm lips parted just a bit, his eyes twinkling with mischief. "I find I can't be serious where you are concerned, my dear. You are far too lovely to be cooped up on this ship, and the ocean air doesn't sit well with your pallor. It should be much more ... rosy. I'm sure I could find a most pleasant way to make it so."

His eyes laughed at his teasing, but he didn't. If he were not such a scoundrel, he'd be too handsome by far, and half the time her foolish heart refused to overlook that fact. All he wanted was money. Her money. Her father had warned her about him before he'd even shown up at the wharf for departure. Shortly after they'd met for the first time in Father's drawing room, Father had told her that Abernathy had lost his family fortune a few years' past in London. He'd been in the states ever since, trying to win it back, without actually working. Marrying her would be a step in the right direction, but she'd been guarded with him from the first and that wouldn't change. It couldn't. But that didn't stop her from coming out to see if Abernathy would grace her with his presence almost every day.

There was also the chance that he didn't want her money at all, but just the thrill of sparring with her until she gave in and let him into her room. He would lose, of course. She had no intention of giving herself to any man, much less Victor Abernathy, rake and gambling fiend.

Since her father would never let her marry a miner and she had no interest in marrying one, either, her prospects in the new little town would be slim—if her father was correct—and he always was. Blessings would be full of miners, and little else. That meant Lenora would remain alone until the little town became more settled, more civilized. She could wait that long and pray for someone who would make her think on her feet, like Mr. Abernathy did. He just had to be a man of character, who wouldn't chase after other women. That would never be tolerated.

"You have nothing to say?" He sighed and frowned dramatically. "Surely, in the long months we've spent together, I've convinced you there's more to me than just what's on the surface. What you can see, and hear, and ... touch."

He reached over and traced her finger with a practiced hand, meant to inflame her very skin. And it worked. His touch was as warm as apple pie and she prayed that Abernathy would tire of his games before he convinced her to believe he *had* changed. There was just no hope in that. But if he did tire of her, would she still come to the rail and hope? She refused to be another conquest for him, just another soft skirt. But where did that leave her? He wasn't bound to keep after her forever. He would tire of their talks and he would find another woman who gave him what he desired. A fleck of worry sparked within her.

"You have done no such thing. I remain certain that the only thing you wish from me is my father's money, and you shall never have it. Excuse me."

Lenora turned to leave his company, but his eyes caught her, and he moved in her path, stopping her like a bird in a cage. Though he did not touch her, she almost wished he would, just to know what it would be like to be held by him. That had to be how he'd tamed so many women; his beautiful, awful eyes, and the desire for his strong arms.

"I want more than your father's money, Lenora Farnsworth. I want your hand, and shall have it. I'm a gambler you see, and I never bet on a hand I might lose."

ABOUT THE AUTHOR

Kari Trumbo is a best-selling author of Christian and sweet romance.

She writes swooney heroes and places that become characters, with historical detail and heart.
She's a stay-at-home mom to four vibrant children. When she isn't writing, or editing, she home schools her children and pretends to keep up with them.

Kari loves reading, listening to contemporary Christian music, singing when no one's listening, and curling up near the wood stove when winter hits. She makes her home in central Minnesota, land of frigid toes and mosquitoes the size of compact cars, with her husband of over twenty years. They have two daughters, two sons, one cat, and one hungry wood stove.

- facebook.com/karitrumboauthor
- twitter.com/KariTrumbo
- instagram.com/karitrumbo
- bookbub.com/authors/kari-trumbo
- goodreads.com/karitrumbo

Made in the USA
Columbia, SC
31 August 2019